LORD'S DOME

E.D.E. Bell

Atthis Arts
Detroit, Michigan

Lord's Dome

This is a work of fiction.

Cover Concept Design by E.D.E. Bell

Cover and Interior Design by G.C. Bell

Published by Atthis Arts, LLC
Detroit, Michigan
atthisarts.com

ISBN 978-1-945009-70-9

First Edition: Published August 2020

This book is dedicated to those who stand with truth.

Truth as truth in context.

Deference to those before.

Strength to those who seek.

Preface

Hello! I'm so glad you've picked up *Lord's Dome*.

I wrote this book in August 2018, during a delay in the editing process for *Diamondsong*. I knew I had longer than I needed to write and submit a short story, but I didn't think I had time to jump into writing the next pieces of the serial, so I decided to try something different and write a short novel. I tried to lean into the short novel form, and combine the skills I'd learned from both multi-genre short stories and fantasy sagas into something interesting. And as always, I tried to write something I'd like to read. I can't call it *completely* spontaneous (I mean, I had one spreadsheet), but for me it certainly was.

I returned to my other projects, and kept running through 2019 and 2020, when (side story: after burning myself out hard and getting helped, over time, back up again) I opened my eyes to find this manuscript. It was interesting to me, used to a more continuous editing process, seeing how much had changed in two years, some things transparent now that seemed forward in 2018, and a few the reverse. (One note: mentions of masks or illness were not written in reference to nor modified in light of the pandemic.) When I showed it to people, they said, go with it, release it now, in fact, the enthusiasm was a boost I needed in what we will all remember as a very difficult year. Without *any* budget (I said it), a team of friends stepped forward to help me smooth it out and send it out, as best we could. The execution was very 2020, a much different experience than the deeper and layered editing of a project like *Diamondsong*.

Yet it ended up fitting with my original goal, which was to not overplan this, and to mostly have fun. I say fun, yet the story itself became rather serious, packed with urgency and *feelings*. I think there can be both? In the jolt an unreal story can provide? And I love to build deep worlds, but for this one, I wanted to tell a story and keep the focus to that. And so, rather than discuss it further here, I'll just let you read it.

I really hope you enjoy it.

Much gratitude goes to the beta team for your thoughtful insights, nudges, encouragement, *friendship*, and so much looking out: Indira Lorick, Tessa Anouska, Jennifer Lee Rossman, Maria Judge, Camille Gooderham Campbell, Sasha Kasoff Moore, Marsalis, Deborah Reilly, and Valerie Linebaugh. And of course to G.C. Bell who knows how this year has been, personally as well, and is still here being passed a piece of paper with doodles for a "Lord's Dome" cover on it and a question if we can release a short novel next month in the middle of finalizing several other projects and is saying "yeah, let's do it" with only occasional arguing. I love all of you. And to anyone reading this book, thanks to you for being open to this odd little story. Now, go. Gu Non has waited long enough.

Godspeed,
E.D.E. Bell
11 August 2020

Yes, because in the sciences, the authority of the opinions of the thousands is not worth a spark as much as the reasoning of one now.

— Galileo Galilei, 01 December 1612

01 About Blue

Gu Non couldn't stop thinking about the magic. They'd lied to her about it. They'd lied to everyone.

No one lied to Gu Non.

She crept through the stone passageways of the mine, following the robed figure. Clumsy, she tripped, and a rock skittered to one side. Holding her breath, she pressed against the jagged wall. Her neck bent forward uncomfortably.

Te Ruk swung around. "Who's there?" he called. "I order you to show yourself." Orders were important here. They maintained function. Safety depended on function. Safety was life.

Gu Non wasn't so great with orders. But she knew what she'd seen, and bad air if she was going to leave before she found the truth of it. Patient, she waited. More patient, she stayed in place when Te Ruk set off again, knowing he'd stop, or turn around suddenly. Mages were smart. But she was smarter.

Pick. Pick. Check.

She left again, watching her feet more carefully now. Staying on the pads of her shoes, she was glad Te Ruk's lamp left a little glow behind it, for she didn't know where she'd find a candle without risking too serious of trouble.

Supplies were so low, even her parents only had one a week for their whole allocation.

The irony of having twelve siblings was that, though they were one of the most making-do families in the mine, they had one of the larger allocations. Almost half of a sleeping dorm, and they only had to share the stove with four families.

Gu Non wondered how many families Te Ruk had to share with. Except, he was clan Mage. They probably had it better. Everyone had it better than clan Mine. Craps, they had to.

No longer seeing the glow of Te Ruk's lamp, she worried she'd let him get too far away. She stumbled in the dark, feeling her way along the cool walls.

At each juncture, she strained to hear the way he'd gone, and she was only mostly sure she'd got it right. Then, she saw the lamp's glow again, and she waited for it to fade before sliding into the large room, staying in the shadows of the corner.

A window! She almost fell over in shock. Grabbing at the wall to steady herself, she gaped at the opening across the room, in what must be an outland chamber.

Light—real, gold light—streamed in through the opening in the stone. Her heart tugged at her, willing her to reach it. What would it be like to stand in the light—would it feel warm or tingly, or would it have a smell? Like all miners, she had to stay between her crew's designated camp and their assigned mining location. And in all of Gu Non's thirteen years, she'd never stood in the light. Not the *real* light.

Irritated, she now understood why. If they let them stand in the light, they'd never return to the dark. Not without a reason. Not without answers.

Te Ruk collapsed against the wall, and he looked like a conjured message as the stream of light shimmered in the dust around him. Except he was not conjured, he was the one to conjure. She'd seen what he did. She'd seen him slip the blue fragment into the pocket of his too-short robes. Because Gu Non saw everything. You know why? Because she *watched*. Mages were given slack, but not so much that he could be here, in what looked like an abandoned camp, with a *core fragment* in his pocket.

Gu Non noticed that Te Ruk did not look well. His hands wrung against each other and his breath was fast. He had not hurried here, so he shouldn't be winded. She sniffed. The air smelled fine. Mages kept the air clean, especially around themselves, so it wasn't that. He was moving again. She refocused.

Te Ruk's shaking hand reached down into the pocket of his robes and pulled out the deep blue stone fragment, which began glowing with azure light. He was touching it with his hands, something *all* were forbidden from doing. Gu Non almost cried out in fear, seeing the blue glow creeping across his fingers, and the drawn agony of Te Ruk's expression.

Her fear turned immediately to fascination, as Te Ruk's body calmed and his eyes closed, and he levitated, just a shin or so above the smoothly cut floor. A flickering sphere of the azure glow grew around him. Eventually, his hand relaxed open, still glowing blue, but now empty. The fragment was gone—consumed, she supposed. Te Ruk lowered to the floor as the bubble around him disappeared.

There.

A lie.

The crew Bosses said the core fragments were burned as fuel, to maintain warmth inside the dome that Lord had built for them, the shield that protected the Varr. The warmth of the furnace replaced the warmth of their star, absorbed by the dome. But they needed the dome for safety from the constant bombardment of the everstorm. And so, the furnace must run. Without constant mining of the mountain's blue core, they would not be protected within the dome until Salvation, when the everstorm cleared and Lord was able to return.

And the mages, granted special powers by Lord to further protect the Varr within the dome, possessed special magic, only granted to those blessed by clan Temple. But the signature azure glow of magic had not come from divine blessing, it had come from the fragment.

Another lie.

Blessing or not, the core stone held the magic, not the mage. And Te Ruk, Gu Non was sure, was using it as a drug.

Eventually, Te Ruk stood and gazed out of the small window. Gu Non tried to imagine what he could see: the beautiful outland, protected by the shimmering glory of the amber dome. She wished she could see it too.

But she had what she needed. And she couldn't be caught here. She had to get to her shift, come up with a plan. Just as she realized Te Ruk was beginning to turn back, Gu Non slipped through the door and tiptoed, later running, until she was back within the safety of her assigned space.

Alarmed at the emptiness of the camp, she ran faster, not wanting more trouble with Ri Wid. Not now, not when she was making her own trouble.

With relief, she saw they were just lining up for shift. Ba Dos was staring out—he sagged a little seeing her, throwing her his "about time" look. She breathed in. She wasn't too late.

"You. Late again." Ri Wid grabbed Gu Non by the hair and swung her back toward the wall, where her shoulder hit a sharp edge. She held her breath to avoid crying out, but Ri Wid took the silence as insolence.

"You think you're above the rules, runt? I have plenty here to make my quota, and a couple more near commission. I don't even need you. There's plenty of spots in controlled labor." He tried to make the sound of a chain being shaken, but it just came out as *ch-ch*. And Gu Non wasn't going to describe how his gesture looked. Didn't need accuracy to make a turd-hearted point, she supposed. The message was loud and clear.

"You so much as pass gas, and this crew will never see you again."

And there it was. Gu Non avoided finding her mother's eyes in the crowd. She knew where they'd be, of course, Ri Wid was staring right at her with his extra-turd-hearted grin. Her mom had turned down his advances, well, pretty much every shift. So he taunted her every chance he got, like the cave slime that he was.

There were plenty of people here that would have serviced him for allocations, really, for almost nothing. But Ri Wid stayed obsessed and wouldn't let it drop. Her mom managed to deal with him, just as they all did. As long as they did their job and followed his rules, he couldn't go too far. At least, not with Te Ruk as their mage. Te Ruk was a lying mage, but he wasn't the worst. Ri Wid was the worst.

She'd deal with him for now. But now that she had her *secret*, one of these days, he'd deal with her.

"Something funny?" Ri Wid had moved in, hovering over her.

"Yes, actually," she answered, immediately regretting the slip. Controlled labor was pure misery, at least by the terrified silence of anyone who came back from it. And Ri Wid absolutely had the power to send her there.

"No, not funny," she amended. "Just grateful that Lord takes care of us. Grateful for another day to serve."

Hearing the words, the whole mining crew repeated them. "Grateful that Lord takes care of us. Grateful for another day to serve."

Ri Wid couldn't interrupt that, and with the moment lost, he threw her a warning glare then proceeded to lead the crew to their mining location.

It was going to be a long shift.

o

The blue stones did not glow as Gu Non chipped them out, in chunks, and loaded them into the carts, cradled in her thick black gloves. Mining the core wasn't like mining rock. It was harder. Core fragments were dense and stubborn, yet if you hit them wrong they'd shatter. Shattered core couldn't be burned as fuel, they said—they were lying, she now knew—so fragments less than four ticks got swept down a chute and didn't count for the quota.

Gu Non was a really crappy miner. She eked by all the time with fragments not even five ticks, while the others loaded large stones, earning Ri Wid's completely fake praise. Fake because he just wanted to be done too, like everyone else. And unlike everyone else, who at least had stones to mine, he just walked around like a sad nothing. Promoted from being a miner, but not blessed like a mage.

Mages were lying about the magic but they weren't just a sad sandwich like Ri Wid was.

Making sure he wasn't watching, she rubbed her arms. She could not draw attention. No more trouble. Not with what she'd decided to do.

Each swing of the mallet onto the pick burned as the shift dragged on. They couldn't leave before the quota, and she hoped to all outland someone was doing well.

Ri Wid's whistle blew. *No!* She wasn't ready!

Frantically, she fumbled at her tools, pretending she hadn't heard. Just as Ri Wid approached, a chunk fell into her glove. By eye, she could tell it wasn't large enough. Three ticks at most.

Spinning around, she rushed to the cart and dipped her glove in. *Crap, crap, crap.*

"What are you doing?" Ri Wid powered toward her,

shaking his counting board. *Ok. Ok.* Except for no warning today, he was usually predictable. *Be predictable now. Please.*

"What size was that?"

She drew her hand back out, shaking under the weight of the core fragment, and desperately hoping she'd picked a good one. It had to make sense.

Ri Wid drew the measurer up from where it dangled around his neck. He whisked the fragment from Gu Non's glove and shooed her back.

"Four ticks. Appropriate, wouldn't you say?" He gave her a nasty smirk.

No, that's it. Be mean. Then let it go. Just like every day. Today's just like every day. Almost too late, she remembered to sully her face. Enough to look like she was irritated, yet trying not to be defiant. Then she forced a smile.

"I hear they have spots in controlled labor," he added with a wink. Gu Non looked down at her boots. Fortunately for her act, the shaking in her hands was very, very real.

"Back to camp," he said, and one by one they lined up to leave.

O

The toilet was a smelly place to be, but it was at least private. She couldn't risk leaving the camp quite yet, not with her mother keeping an extra watch on her, thinking she was up to trouble. See, her mother was smart.

Didn't keep her smart to herself, either. She was still sure Ma Mav was the one who'd started burning the mashhusks that Gu Non and Ba Dos had been sculpting slightly unallowed figures out of. Messed up the whole game. Ma Mav never said a word about it. And neither did Ba Dos, but of course that's what you had a best friend for.

All she had in here was stink and a snuck-out core fragment.

About that.

Without mining gloves, she wasn't quite sure how to loose the fragment from her pocket. Her plan had been to hide a second piece in her offhand glove and slip it into her food box while packing up. But when the whistle blew without a *warning*, all she had for last check was one fragment as small as Ri Wid would have guessed, so she'd just dropped it into her pocket. Then she'd passed check by pretending she'd been trying to drop that one in, when she'd actually grabbed a new one.

The fact that her leg was still doing leg stuff and hadn't turned blue like Te Ruk's hand was a surefine relief.

Of course, the whole thing would have been solved by just trying again next shift. But Gu Non was tired of waiting.

The weirdest part of all this was how easy it had been. Yet, in all her years in the mines, no one had done it. No one had taken a fragment.

Probably because it was punishable by . . . *the thing*.

They didn't say what that meant, obviously, no one was allowed to say it or think it. But what else did it mean to suggest there was a punishment worse than controlled labor? What else did it mean when you heard someone did something really bad and then they never came back? Gu Non knew what never coming back was called, even if they weren't allowed to think it.

With the tunic off entirely, she held it upside down, easing the fragment out. Frustrated, she had to make herself be patient. She couldn't risk it shattering, and if it fell on the ground, it might be hard to pick up again. Slowly, she rolled it out onto her napkin. Hers was old and thin, but it didn't have holes yet. Once it had holes, maybe they'd let her have another one. She needed something for her period, after all.

It was unfair, of course. Most boys got to use their napkins as tissues, or to wipe their mouths, or to tie over a scratch. For the girls, once you started a period, you just used it for that. The girls and Ij Lok too, of course. But Gu Non was clan Mine. She was used to unfair. It could be her clan name. Gu Non Unfair.

She giggled, then realized someone might be in line for the toilet. Well, better to hurry. Taking serious care not to touch the core fragment with her skin, she wrapped it up in her napkin and tied it with a broken bootlace she'd saved. Now secure, she put her tunic back on and picked up the little bundle.

Staring at the stained and tattered napkin with the blue stone inside, she felt a new sense of openness. If she was already in for the worst, then, well, she might as well give this magic thing a try.

02 Up to Trouble

Vo Jie stopped at her doorframe to stretch. With one hand on either side, she leaned in slowly, trying to pull out whatever she'd done to her back.

A throat cleared from inside her room. She jumped back, simultaneously slamming her elbow on the door and pulling something in her shoulder. *Well, that'll be a day to work out.*

"Oh! Are you ok?" A girl leapt up, reaching her hands forward as if she could do something about any of this.

The best thing she could think was at least the twinging pain in her elbow was drowning out what was going to be a very sore shoulder. One-at-a-time pain. Or something. Anyway, what was this child doing in her room?

"Hello, Chief Vo Jie? I'm Gu Non Mine."

This was a child who was up to trouble. She almost laughed at her formal introduction, but that wasn't much fair, since it was required. Yet, of course she was clan Mine; no one who wasn't made any effort to be here on purpose. Except the low-level mages, who had no choice.

She moved to toss the girl out, but, rubbing her shoulder, realized how much risk the young miner had put herself in, being here like this. Bothering a clan Chief was easily punishable, as was being away from camp without permission. Well, then, she'd see what the child had to say. "Have a seat."

"I think I can save all the miners." Smiling, Gu Non sat back onto the floor.

"No, no, here." She pulled a chair over, patting the seat. "Now, save us from what?" Vo Jie tried not to think too hard about what she'd just said.

Gu Non scrunched her face, as she hesitantly moved into the chair. "I . . . I thought it was obvious. We can't keep . . . living the way it is. The air is bad, and Te Ruk Mage can't hardly keep with it. We don't have enough food, and when Te Ruk cures the rot it doesn't always cure right and then people get sick. Bad sick. We can't keep clean because water's so low, and then—well, it can go bad too. And now we're going deeper again? How at?"

She fought the inappropriate urge to correct the child's speech. The miners didn't even get schooling anymore, unless their families took time they hardly had. Well, maybe she had a point. Life hadn't got better in the mines. Vo Jie, she supposed she was used to it. It gave her a pang of regret to see this young girl, refusing to be.

It was also clear what the child was straining so hard not to say. People were dying from infections. Dying from the mines. Dying. Death. Vo Jie didn't care what the rules were; she thought about death often. It was her own silent vigil. The way she'd been able to rebel, in the end. Remembering the dead. Not pretending they never existed. She rested her hand over the locket, hidden under her shirt.

She'd come too close to saying it out loud, though. She needed to be careful. "I understand what you are saying. Conditions in the mine. Well, I know." She felt guilty talking about it. She was probably only alive herself because she'd made her way to Chief. Her work was here, in the room, where she had two candles, a table and two chairs, a private water bin, and her air was on clan Mage's regular patrol. She'd have to move again soon, as they'd all be going deeper with the next rotation.

She knew how it was for the crews. It broke her heart every moment. She did what she could for them, working late hours writing mages' reports for them—and sexual massages for the clan Farm council, too, well, better Gu Non didn't need to know about those yet. Fact was, clan Mine would have half the food they did now without them. Vo Jie did what she could.

"I want you to send me on the deep mission."

Vo Jie's head snapped around, shocked by the request. "A deep mission?" She thought about it. "In place of whom?" There was only one reason someone would ask to go on a deep mission, especially before a new rotation. Maybe to save someone. A family member, she hoped. This one seemed still young for a lover or a child. Too young to know the worst truth of the mines. There was no joy anymore in children. It's why so few were being born. No one wanted to see the child they loved work in the mines, so better not to have them.

"Not in place of anyone. Though—if it saves someone else from going, that would be surefine."

Vo Jie sighed. The girl'd been here long enough, and the way she was talking, one of them would end up in more trouble than clan Mine needed. It was important to think of the others. It was all she did, anymore, really. Her penance for having it so well. She'd do what she could, and then before too long, she'd die.

Except, no one would remember Vo Jie. Rules forbid it. This was fine. Vo Jie didn't deserve to be remembered.

"Gu Non, right? Let me tell you something. You're not supposed to be here. You know that. Yet you're here, putting yourself at risk, asking for my help. And I'm not going to help you based on noble speeches and half-truths. Though I do appreciate the noble speeches; it makes me sentimental. So you tell me what's going on, right now, in a way that I believe you."

Her heart fluttered a bit at the way the child's face steeled. And she knew, she was going to get the truth. Which frightened her, unexpectedly.

"My brother's about to be commissioned. Not the first one: we've got twelve total and I'm near the end. But this one can't go. He's . . . beautiful. And I can't see him in the mines. I can't. For a lot of reasons; it makes me too sad to say them all."

Vo Jie understood that, so she let it pass.

"I think I found a way to fix it. Just the start of a way, but if you pick at a crack long enough, you'll build a passage, right? And if I'm mining all the time, I don't have time to think of it. You'd think I could think mining, but it takes all my concentration, because otherwise I do it wrong and my crew Boss is looking for a reason to send me to controlled labor. So I can't *think* when I'm at work. Not about things that matter."

Well, she was the clan Mine Chief, after all, she didn't need mining explained to her.

"I can fix things. I can. I just need time and space. So the deep mission . . . I'm not going to go on it. They'll think I did, but I'll escape. Once they're deep, they don't come back a bit, and they always pad the crews anyway by a few. I'm terrible at mining; it's a gain if I'm not there. Then I can hide and figure out my plan."

Children could be so perplexing. "Gu Non. What is this plan?"

She took a breath. "Mages don't make magic. The magic comes from the core fragment. If you touch it, you can do magic too. That's what I think. The mages all act really tired or sick. They can barely keep up with air and water down here."

That last part was true, but what had she said? Core fragments create magic? That was more than she could even consider. Lord's blessing creates magic. Not stone. This child was out of control.

"I want to try doing magic myself. Maybe I can figure out how to save us."

Save us. Total blasphemy uttered with the naïveté of youth. Yet, it stirred her, just a little. She would have teared up, if she hadn't learned long ago to prevent such waste.

Her mind spun back to the core fragments. She wanted

to dismiss it, out of hand. They mined for fuel, not magic. And she didn't want this girl touching a core fragment.

"If you touch a fragment—" She couldn't say *you'll die.* But she would. It was why guidelines were so strict for their handling.

"I saw Te Ruk with one. He touched it in his bare hand, and he used it up."

What? Vo Jie sat down. The girl was not lying. There was no lie in her face. But then, thinking through it, the mages had lied to her all her life. All her life. A lie.

Gu Non sat, waiting for her answer.

Vo Jie hardened her gaze. "I'll file the orders. Discover whatever you need. Do not come back here. I . . . I wish you well."

The girl stood, but hesitated. "My brother is Da Eel," she added. "You asked for all the truth."

All the truth.

Disoriented, she watched as the girl smiled, bowed, and marched out into the passage. This was going to take her time to understand. Her thoughts weren't as fast as they once were; she'd long since accepted that.

She'd once been like young Gu Non, she admitted to herself. It's why she'd worked so hard to get here. Younger than any of the other crew Bosses, then a Scheduler, then clan Chief. With each step, she'd felt no grander than before. Just more burdens. More helplessness, knowing the whole clan was angry with her, and she'd not done enough to fix it.

She'd not known how.

Vo Jie still thought about death. She even carved the word sometimes in the ashes before sweeping them away. She wondered if Gu Non knew the word, or just the idea.

She thought about her own brother, who'd complained of not being well. But Vo Jie was a crew Boss, and they'd been behind. She'd asked if he could help. Instead, he'd tripped on a lever and been crushed by a cart. They'd carried off his body and he was never mentioned again. It never happened. Lord values life, they said. It was the only reminder offered to what else must not be discussed.

The best she could do to honor him was remember that he had lived. Or so she'd thought.

Maybe she could do more.

Magic came from core fragments? This basic premise so dismantled everything she'd ever done, that it could not be true.

Her hand tapped the locket. An old locket, secretly passed down through her family. An illegal item now. Even more so for being filled with her brother's hair. Hair she'd cut from his dead body, before it ceased to exist.

She hadn't been able to protect him.

Vo Jie jumped from her seat and to her files. Flipping through, she found the registration. Gu Non. Crew 71. Walking briskly enough that her cough started to bother her, Vo Jie hurried down the corridors toward their camp. Around a bend, she almost ran into the child.

Not alone, Gu Non's crew Boss was leaning over her, beaming like he'd been given a prize.

"Chief," he said, stepping back.

"Yes, I need a miner for a bit and I was hoping to find a Boss who could— Oh, who's this? This one looks strong; she'll do. Come, this way. Oh," she turned back to the Boss. "You can spare her, of course? Your crew isn't short? I need more for a deep mission. Which crew's this one from?"

The Boss almost laughed, but he turned it into a nasty little snort. "Crew 71," he chortled. "You can definitely have her." He winked at Gu Non.

And with that, her desire to help solidified. Even if the girl was delusional. Her delusions were better than their reality, she figured.

Not taking her hand from Gu Non's arm, she marched her back into her room and swung her into the closet, one that was kept lit, not brightly but enough, by one of the mage pipes running through it.

"I own you now, do you understand? You follow every rule I give you. Starting with you stay in this room unless I give you permission to leave. The air is good here; it's cleaned by the mage pipe." She pointed up. "It's always lit but you'll get used to it. Now, your guardian—can they be trusted? Only to tell them you're well. And to pull what we can from your bedding."

Gu Non seemed to hesitate. "I have two. A mother and a father. My mother can be trusted. My father . . . this place got to him. We'd best not."

Vo Jie nodded. "I'll get a message to your mother."

03 A New Mage

It took Vo Jie *forever* to leave her room. Finally, Gu Non heard the creak of the door. Just in case it was a trick to see if she was going to break the rules Vo Jie had set, Gu Non waited another several minutes. Hearing nothing, she crept out into Vo Jie's room.

She paused to stare at the expansive, private space. Big enough to fit four more beds, Vo Jie had a separate room with a table, two chairs, and three large boxes with knobs in little rows. The boxes were as tall as Gu Non!

She touched one of the knobs, but nothing happened. It turned against her fingers, but this looked far too large and fancy for a fidget. With a tug, the wood scraped out, stopping in protest as it hit a side. Delighted, she wiggled two knobs at the same time, and found that it was like a hidden box, housing rows and rows of paper records.

Well, this was too much prying for someone who had helped her out. Even if she could read them. She closed the box by pushing the knobs back in.

That said, no one owned Gu Non. She stamped on the floor a little to make the point. Not even her clan Chief who seemed pretty nice every time she'd visited their camp, which was why she'd trusted her in the first place. And she was grateful to have Vo Jie's large closet all to herself, but she wasn't going to *stay* in it. How could she fix everything by staying?

She closed her own room's door—imagine having her own door—and slipped out into the passage, closing Vo Jie's door and getting away before anyone could see her. Her napkin was already wrapped around the core fragment, but she still had her sick tie. Wrapping it around her face and tying it in the back, she made it look like she was really sick, and pulled the thing almost up to her eyeballs. With that and tucking her hair into her mining cap, she could be anyone. Anyone her size, she supposed. And no one even looked at her, no one wanted to, as she wove between the camps and past them, into a blue-lit corridor.

Just as she hoped, Te Ruk was alone in his room. She knew which room belonged to clan Mage, she'd figured that out right after she realized he was taking core fragments. Miners weren't allowed back here, but anyway. Taking a quick moment to make sure he wasn't doing anything embarrassing, she walked in and shut the door.

Reaching an important point where she could have shaken down the mage, she again made herself pause to gaze at the *room* they gave this guy. And he wasn't sharing it with *anyone*. As far as she knew, he was kind of a crappy mage, yet this place was like Lord's Eternal Palace. Well, that at least would have had a window.

She still wasn't over seeing that window. When she found the time, she'd have to go back there.

Te Ruk's room was at least twice the size of Vo Jie's. And

where hers was surrounded by those wood boxes, Te Ruk's had shelves that weren't even being used: they were just dotted with old-looking figures and a few thin books. He had two doors in the back of the room, each closed. There were metal tubs, maybe with water in them? And a soft smell didn't remind her as much of the mine. She didn't know what it was, except that it was nice.

Except, she was here to shake down the mage. And, she reminded herself, she had her own room now too. No sharing. Kinda like a mage too, she grinned to herself, under the fabric. So she took off the sick tie and shoved it in her pocket. And the mining cap too, because she despised wearing it anyway.

"How dare you?" Te Ruk leapt up from a chair. *A* chair. He had *four.*

"I know you take core fragments." Gu Non jutted her jaw forward. On purpose. To show him she wasn't afraid.

Te Ruk sat back down.

"Not only do I know you *take core fragments,*" she continued, "I saw you use one. For magic. Now," her voice softened, "I do understand you seem to have some problems. So I'm not trying to be mean, and I don't like trouble for anyone. But I want to start by having an understanding here about what I know. And, if you tell anyone I was here, what I can tell the priests."

Feeling bold, Gu Non swung out a chair and sat in it backward, her legs angling out awkwardly from each side. "I'm Gu Non Mine. I'm she."

Te Ruk stared at her a very long while. Enough that

Gu Non thought maybe she was too late, and Te Ruk had already crossed into some magic zone or something. Then he laughed.

"Do you know what I could have done to you before you even got a chance to tell your little story? That no one would believe?"

Thinking this was rather funny, Gu Non laughed too.

"What would you have done? Send me deep into the caves, where I already am? Where I'll end up anyway. Where I have no *rule-following* way to get out? What would you make me do? Chip rocks all shift while a bully says nasty things to us? Then go back and rest in a cramped dorm until I have to do it again? Is that what you would do to me? Or is it . . . worse?" She laughed, thinking of Ri Wid's silent threat that they could leave and never come back. "Anything worse you could do to me would only cause me fewer shifts."

She'd gone a little far there. Almost implying *the thing*. Well, Ri Wid implied it to them all the time; they just weren't allowed to think about it. But seriously, what was he threatening? What could he do to her that was worse than this? Da Eel needed her. She'd do what she needed.

He stood up from the table, and with alarm, Gu Non noticed that he didn't look well. Didn't look steady. Rounding the table and getting right in her face, she noticed he was reaching for his pocket. Would he?

Suddenly the idea of having nothing to lose felt a little exaggerated.

As his hand plunged into his robe, a blue glow began to

emerge, and now, face-to-face, Gu Non did the only thing that seemed smart.

She grabbed her fragment too.

Wrenching the little tie from the napkin, her hand thrust out from her pocket, and stunned, she saw her fingers turning blue, glowing with the same light. His eyes widened, and he no longer looked like the harmless mage she'd come here to confront.

Gu Non was shocked too.

"Lord, protect me," she whispered, out of instinct.

Just as Te Ruk's hand crackled with some sort of furious bolt, a bubble of light surrounded Gu Non. Shimmery, like the descriptions of Lord's Dome, she could see Te Ruk's wild eyes staring through it. But her shield was not gold, it was a dark metallic color, like the stone surrounding them. With sparks of blue and an energy around it, like rippling water. Its edges crackled with whatever had shot from Te Ruk's hand.

Through it, she could see him raise his hand again.

She turned and ran.

At each turn, she went another forbidden direction. As forbidden as she could go, for now. For she could not be seen, not be followed, not be recognized—not surrounded by shimmery metal light and being chased by clan Mage. Not while breaking the most important rule of the mines.

Core fragments must never, ever be touched.

Images flashed in her mind, not visual images, but feelings, snippets of thoughts.

Protect them. Protect them. Protect them.

What? She tried to push them away, but they were inside her. Talking in her mind. Little tickles from deep inside her, an itch she couldn't quite scratch. She'd deal with that when she could.

The bubble followed her down each passage, through an old, abandoned section, where images of protection continued to fuel her shield, caused it to grow and strengthen, until she almost couldn't see through it.

Whatever was playing in her mind still wouldn't stop. *Tradition doesn't matter,* they said. They didn't care what tradition was. *Protect them.*

Finally, she hit a full stop, a pocket of emptiness, where every fragment that could be reached from the camps had been chipped away, and they'd retreated to mine a new path, somewhere deeper.

Out of breath, she collapsed, staring at the blue tint slowly fading away, at first illuminating the broad, hollow space but then fading to darkness. Something had been in her mind. *In her mind.* She didn't like that at all.

She didn't even know whether to feel good about what had happened, or terrible. She'd failed, overall. She'd used up her only core fragment, the one she'd risked everything to get. She'd made Te Ruk an enemy without even getting to ask him about the core fragments or the magic. She'd just gone in and made him mad. That couldn't help.

Yet, she'd used the magic. She'd proven she could, that maybe anyone could—being a mage wasn't a condition for magic, it was the result. And she'd proven her theory that magic came from the core, not from Lord's blessing.

Unless she had Lord's blessing too and didn't know it, but that was still the same point. She was clan Mine! Not clan Mage. Those mages were truly lying!

And in her mind, a new feeling had entered. Not a new feeling, because she wanted to protect Da Eel; it was why she'd taken the core. But it was the strongest feeling she'd ever felt—an urgency to protect something more important than anything else in existence.

I will not back away!

A final thought stung her mind as the magic faded. That . . . whatever was gone, right? She wasn't sure. Something . . . something stayed with her. She tried to ignore it. Returning her sick tie and cap, she stuck her hand into the pocket, really sad that she'd lost her only napkin. But she couldn't let anyone see her hands, not if there was any blue glow left to them.

It took her a while to find her way back in the dark. She was good at memorizing turns, but she'd been hurrying so much when she ran away, she hadn't caught them all. Finally, she reached the active area, where the lamps again lit the passages. Her fingers shook from within her pocket, and turned each corner with relief now, hoping to get back out of sight.

Was Te Ruk looking for her? He wouldn't know about Vo Jie, though. She was just some girl from a crew; she didn't think he'd go all the way to Vo Jie about her. But, she didn't know the mage at all.

Running when alone, and slowing to a permitted hurry as she passed others, she burst into Vo Jie's room, nearly collapsing to see it still empty. Staggering into her closet, she breathed in the clean air supplied by the mage pipes, standing on her tip toes for a few minutes to get the full blast of it. Her breath finally calming, she leaned back against the wall.

Unable to process everything she'd felt, she was glad for a while to be not allowed to go anywhere else. That was just in her mind, of course. Rules were just things people agreed to do. And Gu Non agreed, she just didn't need to talk to anyone else for a little while.

The phantom pain she felt from whatever had invaded her mind still haunted her. What was it protecting? What was it?

Lord, what was that?

There was no answer.

Gu Non stared at the wall.

04 In Too Deep

Hearing a slight shuffle from the closet, Vo Jie was glad Gu Non had had the sense to stay put. She'd filled out her orders, and the deep mission crew would be leaving before next shift. She'd filled out half the orders, she should say. Gu Non's previous Boss had orders she'd been taken away, and her supposed new Boss wouldn't know to look for her.

In some sense, Gu Non now only existed in this room.

She still had no idea what the girl wanted to do, but maybe Vo Jie could at least talk to her now. Keep her from doing anything rash.

Opening a drawer, she slid Gu Non's phantom orders down into a pocket. The drawer pushed shut.

Untying her wrap, Vo Jie winced as the bandage rubbed a bit against her upper arm. She'd had the wound, a nasty thing, for two years now, but even with access to the best balm from clan Farm, it wouldn't close. It was these conditions, of course. Bad air, no rest, poor food—she wasn't sure which of it.

Vo Jie was tired.

Still, life was precious, she reminded herself. Sponging off the wound, she wrung the stained bandage in the water. With a final squeeze, she went to dry the bandage in the mage light to reuse it, but then remembered Gu Non was in the closet. That's fine, she had another cloth, and wouldn't bother the girl.

Instead, she hung the stained cloth to dry in the air, and reached up to a shelf to find a dry cloth, only with a couple holes. She brought it down and layered it around the wound. Even the relatively smooth fabric felt harsh and cruel over the raw flesh, but it was better than having it rub on loose clothing, or stain her already-tattered wrap.

Gingerly, she tied her shirt back on, just as a rapping sounded at the door.

"Come in," she offered, just before remembering Gu Non was still there. Well, hopefully the child had sense to stay quiet. She hoped whoever was here wouldn't wonder why the closet door was closed. She normally kept it open, to have benefit of the mage light inside.

There weren't too many people left in the mines who'd feel comfortable calling on a clan Chief. But she didn't have much time to wonder which it would be. Te Ruk, their current assigned mage, peeked in through the opening door, sweat across his brow.

Thinking of it, she hadn't talked to the mage in a while. And, oh, he didn't look well at all. Maybe Gu Non had more of a point than she'd realized. He set down his own lamp, which caused the room to glow with azure-tinted light. Then closed the door behind him.

"Te Ruk, please," she said, pulling out her guest chair. She'd said it loud enough that just in case Gu Non hadn't caught the knock at the door, she'd realize now there was company.

"Chief Vo Jie Mine," he said, taking the offered seat.

"Te Ruk Mage," she said with a curt nod, joining him.

"You're helping the child. Gu Non."

It was turning out to be a strange day. "A child in the mine? I help them all, however I still can."

Te Ruk's head twitched, tilting oddly against his neck. Though they'd never had much of a relationship, Vo Jie's concern for the man grew. She knew not to grow attached to the mages; getting out of the mines was always their priority.

"I heard about the orders. Next deep mission. Right when her Boss was threatening to send her to controlled labor."

Controlled labor! She didn't know that. As much hardship as Vo Jie had seen, she was not so hardened to ignore the image of the sharp-eyed child being sent to work in chains. She'd seen it before, but there were so few children now. They couldn't even protect the last few.

"I am not aware that the mages make mine assignments their business," she replied.

Te Ruk leaned forward, an unsettled flicker to his eyes. "You don't know what it does to you. Chief—"

There was clearly something he wanted to say about Gu Non, something he couldn't push out. Well, there were really only three things that couldn't be discussed here: death, magic, and leaving. Given that the child had agreed to live in her closet, it was most likely— Well, that's what she had said, wasn't it? That she would do magic.

Oh. And she had. She could see it in Te Ruk's twitching

lip. This little game was getting more dangerous by the moment. Vo Jie remembered her signature on the orders.

"Please," he continued, "she doesn't know what she's doing."

That comment struck a nerve. No one knew anything these days; they'd shut down the schools for necessity, but even what could be shared wasn't. All that mattered was life. Day after day of life. Mining the core for life. Never mind the how. "Who does know, Mage? How is it our fault to be kept in ignorance when clan Mage has worked so hard to keep us there?"

Stunned at her own words, Vo Jie realized she'd probably just lost her position as Chief. And likely worse. Controlled labor. Death, even. She sat up taller.

"What does she want?" he asked, his words shaky.

"To help us," Vo Jie answered. "With this," she swung her hand in an arc.

"I tried to warn her," Te Ruk said. Without explaining it, he sat something small onto the table. Then, his face growing cold and plain, he rose, turned, and left, closing the door again behind him.

By rote, Vo Jie had risen at his departure. Her legs faltered as she lowered back into her chair. She suddenly didn't like the idea of sitting here alone. "Child, come out here," she said, hoping she couldn't be heard from the corridor but too unnerved to stand.

The door pushed open, and Gu Non's face appeared through the opening. How had she managed to get grubby already, just sitting in one place. Children.

Glancing around, well, she must have heard Te Ruk's voice, she tentatively joined Vo Jie at the table. Gu Non was fixed on the item that Vo Jie had almost forgotten he'd left there. It looked like a napkin. As Gu Non picked it up, she saw it was two. Entirely new fabric. Without comment, Gu Non took them and slid them into her pocket, a starved look in her eyes as if it had been food.

"I have come to a decision," Vo Jie said, an idea occurring to her in that moment. "If each day here, you can tell me you are closer to what you seek, I will let you stay. If you are not, then I cannot allow this danger to pass. For any of us."

It was not truly a threat, for she could see Gu Non was accustomed to threats. Instead, it was a risk. She could see the spark, not yet taken from the child. Vo Jie's spark had gone out long ago.

"I made progress today, Chief Vo Jie."

That that comprised the report amused her. Though, she supposed, it met her requirement. Like any good miner. Complete what you are assigned. Rest. Do it again. It would be nice, for a while, to think in a different way.

"Tell me about your brother," she tried, deciding whatever the story was with the napkins, she didn't need to know.

"He is Da Eel Mine. He likes to draw, and he's good at inventing puzzles. He cries a lot, but he smiles a lot too. I like to play with him; he invents games using stones and scraps. He thinks . . . differently than the rest of us do." Her face fell, just as it had brightened at his first mention. "He's about to be commissioned, as I said, but he's not prepared for it. Ri Wid is cruel, and Da Eel has a true heart." Gu Non looked up as if begging Vo Jie to understand. And she did.

For a moment, Vo Jie considered telling Gu Non about her own brother. But as there was no way to speak of the dead without acknowledging death—and she wasn't going to pretend he was out reclanned in the outland or any nonsense—so instead she rose to steep some herbs. She placed one sprig into each of two mugs as Gu Non looked on with interest.

"Your cups have handles," Gu Non admired, a smile breaking on her face.

"Yes," Vo Jie said. Did clan Mine no longer provide handles, even? She poured water into each.

"What do you know about the core?" Gu Non asked, her eyes still affixed to the steeping drinks.

The response came to mind: To fuel the furnace. The furnace was used to heat the inside of the dome, to enable farming while the Varr stayed protected by Lord's Dome from the everstorm above. But Gu Non knew that answer already. Her answer, then, was embarrassing.

"I don't know. I was born here, like you. Life was different then, but also the same." It was more than that, though. They'd always been told the core fueled the furnace. That was all there was to it, and so there were no questions to ask. What, then, was special about this one youth, who asked questions into darkness, seeking justification for decree?

"You've lived here so long though," Gu Non said,

turning back toward Vo Jie. "We need the core to heat the dome, right? So why is there a dome?"

"To protect us from the everstorm."

"Why is there an everstorm?" Gu Non leaned in.

"From evil."

"If Lord protected us from evil with a dome, why didn't he fight the evil? Or warm the dome?"

Vo Jie had no answers. And Gu Non wasn't done.

"And where are the priests, to allow us to ask these questions? To help us understand why we must suffer for so long. Why my brother must suffer."

Understand. Vo Jie knew that was a dangerous word. To a priest, understanding equaled faith. Not questions.

"So that's my next step, then. I'll need to talk to the priests." She leaned back in the chair.

At a loss for words, Vo Jie removed the herbal sprigs, and placed the two cups on the table. She stared at the cups. And took a breath. "Do not talk to the priest," she finally said. A couple of miners couldn't withstand that sort of spotlight; they'd be better working alone.

"Why not?"

Vo Jie felt that was obvious, but if she needed to—

"If clan Temple exists to understand Lord, and I have questions about Lord, why wouldn't I talk to the priests of clan Temple? All that studying has to be for something, right? Otherwise, why aren't they down here mining? What else are they for?"

She'd never thought of it that way. She'd clearly never thought of a lot of things. Of course, who remembered what notions she'd had at Gu Non's age. She'd learned, though. The hard way. And if that's what Gu Non was headed for, Vo Jie had no idea why she continued to help her. Why she would help her fan a cruel hope that would only lead to sorrow.

"Chief Vo Jie?" The girl leaned forward.

Vo Jie looked up.

"When you said that you owned me, I know that's because you aren't used to breaking rules. So I'm not mad, but I need you to know that I know that's not true either."

Vo Jie opened her mouth and closed it again. Her thoughts now fully in a jumble, she walked to her cabinet. The filter grains were getting low, here and in the storage too. She supposed she was due another visit to clan Farm. Time to think, as Gu Non had wanted.

For today, there was enough to pour two full portions. For reasons she couldn't pinpoint, she felt they deserved them.

"Well, let's eat, then."

"I used the magic, Vo Jie. And I'm going to do it again." She stared back with an expectant gaze.

"I know, Gu Non."

The child smiled back, brighter than before.

As Vo Jie stirred the grains, thinking maybe she could spare a little of her remaining fungi to season them, she considered how nice it was to have company again. And— how much trouble they'd both be in when they were caught.

05 Bitter

Drawing was not Gu Non's best talent. She'd found the paper in a scrap bin—she had no idea what it said but it was so official they'd left the other side blank—and if she scratched the rock just right, it would leave a gray outline without ripping the paper.

Not ripping the paper wasn't as hard as getting these drawings to make sense.

Vo Jie had even left Gu Non's door open today— Gu Non wasn't sure what that was about, but Vo Jie had left the room anyway, so she'd closed the door while she was working on the note. Sometimes thinking needed to be alone. Her father used to say that, long ago when he said nice things. He didn't say nice things anymore. She wasn't mad at him, though. Only sad.

She'd put together a sequence fit for Lord's Book, though, she thought with pride. The people weren't really the right shape, but they were clearly people. What else would they be? She drew a triangle on top of Te Ruk's body. Mage robes. He'd get that.

In the first frame, she'd drawn him holding two squares. Those were napkins. And there a heart above them, because her period would have been a nightmare without a napkin, and this one was thick and strong—she was pretty sure it was new. Like full-up outland new.

The curious point was the *second* napkin. Either he just was used to having extra things in clan Mage and didn't know that was wasteful, or he was sending her a message. The message could be that her face was dirty, but she didn't like that one, so she was going to ignore it. The other message could be that he knew she needed something to carry a core fragment in, without danger of accidentally touching it. He hadn't replaced the string she'd used, but there were string scraps right here in Vo Jie's closet.

My room, she corrected.

And if he'd given her a napkin to carry a core fragment, well then, he wasn't opposed to her trying the magic again. She hadn't really thought through how she was going to get more fragments—it wasn't as if she could approach a mining crew without putting people in big danger—but now she had an idea.

Under the thank you picture, she drew Te Ruk again. This time, he was handing her a little circle. He'd know it was her, not just because she made that person small, but she put a mining pick in one hand and added some little lines coming out of the other. Hopefully that wasn't too far. And then, for extra flair, she'd added a dotted square in the pocket, like she was carrying a new napkin, she giggled.

The trick was whether he'd understand the message. She'd drawn him passing over a *circle* to her, because that didn't mean anything. It wasn't as if she could draw a core fragment; what if someone saw it?

She folded the paper, and rolling a ball of old oil she'd scraped from one of Vo Jie's empty jars, she sealed it shut.

Walking around was a risk, but she hoped between her sick tie, her cap, and her very sneaky ability to be smart and avoid people, she could still go out when she needed to. She made it all the way back to Te Ruk's room without anyone seeming to notice.

Her ear pressed against the closed door. No voices sounded inside. Giving the little paper a kiss, or whatever was written on its outside, she slid it under the door and scooted away as fast as she could.

The next stop would be harder. But, if she had measured it right, her whole crew ought to be on shift now. Hopefully no one was back sick today. Ducking through her camp and into her old living space, she was glad to see Da Eel, playing alone.

"Hey, it's me," she said, stopping to pull him into a big hug.

Emotional, Da Eel pressed his lips together.

"It's ok, you don't have to talk if it's too much right now. I wanted you to know that I'm ok, and I'm trying to help us." She didn't want to say more than that; it wouldn't be nice to get his hopes up. But she didn't want him to be sad either. "I'm just going to live somewhere else for a little while. I won't see you for a bit, but I am ok."

Protect them.

Whatever comfort she would have taken from seeing the relief in her brother's face was erased as the creepy voice reentered her mind. *Get out,* she replied. *Besides, I'm trying to and you're bothering me.*

Da Eel had started to talk, but seeing her face, he'd stopped, drawing back. "Gu Non?" he whispered.

"Sorry, just sort of a burpy thing."

He smiled.

"Here, what games have you invented?"

Da Eel scrambled to the side of the room, where he pulled out a bag of stones and started to arrange them. Sometimes Da Eel's games were too complex for Gu Non to understand, but as long as she played with him, he never seemed to mind.

"Do you have any food?" he asked. This broke Gu Non's heart, every time he asked it. He was hungry here. He was always hungry. So were they all. But Da Eel didn't seem to accept that allocations were allocations, and there was no extra food to be had.

Maybe that strange voice was doing something to her, but Gu Non was starting to feel the same way. She wanted to protect Da Eel, and she would do anything to do it. Even if it meant the magic might bring back that other world.

In fact, if she was here to be serious about it, maybe she just needed to get back there. Hopefully Te Ruk came through and brought her fragments. Whether he really cared, or whether she'd frightened him, well she'd rather he cared, but the point was she was doing this no matter what.

Another look at Da Eel's thin arms and she knew there was no other choice. Not for her, anyway. She sunk herself into playing whatever game Da Eel had created, and almost didn't realize how late it had become. But she heard voices coming their way.

With a quick hug to Da Eel and a reminder that she was ok, even if he didn't see her, she rushed back out, turning the corner from the camp.

Fear gripped her just as a hand did, preventing her from running past. Turning in terror, she almost cried out to see her mother's, well, not exactly friendly face.

"Ma Mav," she whispered. "I have to go."

"You can't come back here like this. I know you care about him, but if you're trying something, you have to try it on your own. You can't drag him into it."

"Ma Mav, you don't understand." Her mother didn't seem to appreciate Gu Non's words. She tried to fix it. "I mean, I'm trying something."

"Gu Non. I know I can't stop you." She glanced over her shoulder, sadness taking her face. "And I wouldn't try. But you can't come back here. It puts him at risk. It puts *you* at risk. Do you understand me? Gu Non. *Please.*"

She didn't want her here? Fine. Gu Non didn't need to be where she wasn't wanted. "Ok. Fine. If you promise you'll keep telling him I'm ok."

Her mother's lip twisted. "I promise."

"Good," she answered, shaking loose of her mother's grip. "But here's my promise. I will protect Da Eel. No matter what."

"Never say no matter what."

She didn't know how to answer that. Didn't her mother trust her? Thinking of how to explain, she suddenly realized she was alone. Throwing her sick tie and cap on as best she could, she darted back, keeping her head down and hoping no one bothered to look. With relief, she waited for the main hall to empty, then ran down it, spinning back into Vo Jie's room.

Glad Vo Jie was not there, she ran into her room and shut the door. A bundle sat in the middle of the floor. Wrapped in a whole piece of fabric, it was painted with green crossmarks: the symbol of sickness. Normally depicting something that had been exposed to a serious illness and must be burned, Gu Non understood. Taking a pair of gloves from Vo Jie's shelf, she pried open the package.

Several core fragments, none as large as four ticks, but still several, rested in a pile. This was a *lot* of core fragment. Shocked that he'd really done it, she pulled the whole pile into a corner and sat a bucket over it.

Te Ruk was willing to help her. Vo Jie was willing to help her. Yet her own mother had turned her away. Lectured her. Told her not to visit her little Da Eel. This was wrong. It was all wrong.

Bitterness overtook her, and ready to learn whatever there was to learn, she lifted the bucket, plunging her hand in to grab a blue stone. As before, it glowed as the bucket clattered back over the rest.

Falling against the shelves and ignoring the pain in her back, the bitterness inside her grew.

There is no return.

Somewhere, in this world, an inherent bitterness filled her. They would continue to engage in this conflict. Nothing would stop it. Nothing would resolve it.

Is this what you wanted? Was this worth it?

I have failed you.

Bitter. Bitter. Bitter.

Gu Non wallowed in it. She drank it. She despaired, and it felt like a thousand years inside her.

Nothing can stop this.

Lord would always be bitter.

She sat up in her seat. *Lord. Lord? God of all life? This was Lord in her head?*

Yes, of course it was. She knew that now, with all certainty.

Her mind shook, as though she were skipping back and forth between awake and asleep. Not sleepy, but back and forth. Conscious. Away. Here. Not. Forcing her mind back together, she focused on the room around her.

If these were Lord's thoughts, were they happening right now? Was she hearing Lord right now? Or was it a prophecy maybe, like in one of Ma Mav's stories?

No, she knew it was not a vision. It was a memory. The emotions were too powerful to be anything *but* memory. Stories could be powerful, but only when memory helped create them. The priests told them always to pray. She tried it now.

"Lord," she whispered. "I guess you're upset about the everstorm. Yeah, it's wrecking us pretty hard. But I won't be mad at you if you can just come back and help us. I know you're waiting for it to be over, and I don't understand god-problems. But if you come back, I found some magic here and maybe we can work together. Please let me know. Thanks. Gu Non."

She hoped that's how you did it.

As the room returned around her, she realized her legs shook in a scary way, and her tongue felt dry. Looking back to make sure the bucket covered the rest of the fragments, she stumbled out and drank more than she ever had in one sitting, grateful for Vo Jie's large water bin.

Trying to regain her sense of the world and push aside Lord's bitterness, which had right away pushed aside her own, she grasped at her own thoughts, finally centering in on one.

She needed to visit clan Temple.

There was usually one priest forced to visit the mines. Gu Non would skip him. No one here knew anything. Not Vo Jie, not Te Ruk. What would a low-level priest know.

Then, it was time for Gu Non to visit the outland.

Able to shake her mind clear for one moment, she thought, *I am finally going to stand in the light.*

06 Maybe She Had a Point

Vo Jie had spent years convincing herself that the situation could not be changed, and that her best guard against complete misery was to help as many people as she could while she lived, and someday sigh with relief into the final darkness when it took her.

Gu Non had ripped this shroud away with the cruelty of youth, leaving her with only the worst of both worlds: a sad old woman who realized she'd probably lived a lie.

Yet, this didn't defeat her the way it might have, she mused. Like an intoxicant, or maybe just fresh air, she opted instead to breathe it. Gu Non's questions had been circling in her mind. Especially the one about clan Temple.

Most priests avoided the mines as much as Lord would allow them, but some poor fellow would always be sent here, usually to check on clan Mage, often meditating in seclusion and counting the days until he could return. This was fine, Vo Jie avoided them too.

It was a bit of a walk to where the priests stayed; they never built their space too close to the active camps, preferring to stay back one or two rotations. Walking through the passages gave her an odd sense. It wasn't so far away from where she lived, yet she never walked here. Just stayed in the small space where she was supposed to be.

Orders. Rules. They were easy to fall into. And it was jarring to do something new, even if just walking down an empty passage, her small lamp's gold light bouncing against its silvery walls.

And so she found the clan Temple door was left open, and by his dress and posture, the man inside clearly expected no company. *What a sad life,* she couldn't help but think. All that wealth and privilege, yet here he was, alone in this empty, abandoned space. Not leaving it the way she hadn't left hers.

Though, he did have a couch with padding, she noted. While their infirm slept on towels. She pursed her lips, unable to remember the last time she'd seen a couch in the mines.

"Hello," she said, rapping the open door. The man jumped so high she again felt sorry for him. For a second, anyway.

"Lord's blessing," he spouted, hopping around and brushing himself off.

"I am Vo Jie Mine," she said with a bow. "I am she." The priest would of course be he; all priests were, in Lord's image. She left her own honorific off. There was no rank when talking to clan Temple. She was only the highest of the very low, even here.

"Ny Auv Temple," he said, looking unsure about something. Finally, he issued a low nod. Vo Jie almost laughed.

The man didn't look too concernedly zealous, she noted. He was supposed to be in Temple robes, but instead he had a soft gray sleeping robe and a light, shawl-like wrap. His white hair fell over a balding head, soft strands of hair that hadn't been cut for a while, as opposed to being intentionally long. His eyes were a little lopsided and his thin lips struggled to form a smile.

I suppose seniority doesn't keep you from the mines. Well, look at herself. It was all relative.

There was no sign he'd seen a visitor lately, though she almost asked whether Gu Non had been there. She stopped, seeing in his expression she had not. No one had. Well, that was one good thing, anyway. Maybe the child had reconsidered.

"Please, take a seat," he offered. "I don't have much else here. We, um, drink our own beverage. But it's safe, if I could get you a cup."

More important than the unsettling sound of this beverage was Vo Jie's sense he wasn't really supposed to offer it to anyone outside of his clan. "You can't drink anything else?" She wasn't sure why she was being so rude. After all, it was rare to find anything other than water these days.

He cleared his throat. Vo Jie, realizing he probably wasn't supposed to talk about that either, could not say why she felt an urge to save him from the embarrassment. "It would be nice to try it," she corrected. "If it won't do anything too suspicious?" Vo Jie had been around people a long time, and she sensed no deceit.

"No, no." He walked to a lidded pitcher and rummaged around to find an additional cup. Suddenly, he turned around. "Can we try this again?"

They both laughed.

"I mostly talk to my clipboard myself, so I'd say we don't worry."

"Sure," he answered, smiling. "Well, it's what I have. They get funny if we don't stick to it. Yes, I know they aren't here to see, but if I can't live for my own integrity, I don't know if I have much else."

"I understand," she said. She did.

The drink was almost water anyway—the Temple must be deluding themselves with visions of grandeur—but it did have a slight flavor of something familiar. There was a bit of herb, but something else. Maybe, a dried citrus? Very slight.

"It's good," she said, setting down the cup.

They stared at each other across the table.

Vo Jie was used to dealing with people in power. Offering them what they wanted in exchange for what she needed. This was different. What life had led this man to sitting alone in an empty room with more wealth than anyone in her clan?

And why were they all just going along with it?

He had to be wondering why she was there.

"How nervous do I need to be about you turning me in somewhere if you don't like what I have to say?" she asked, realizing that if he wanted, he could have her punished just for that. For anything, really.

He took a sip. "Not nervous. I've— Please. I enjoy the company."

Irony upon irony. All he had to do was walk to the camps. People would have flocked to him, hoping for favor.

Vo Jie was tired of all of it. In that moment, she stopped fretting. Whatever would happen would happen.

"Does Lord speak to you?" Vo Jie didn't mean to be rude. She was curious also.

"He . . . Lord is away. Until the everstorm clears." He shifted in his seat.

"If he is all-powerful, why doesn't he clear the everstorm? Or tell us how to leave it? Or send aid?"

"He aided us with his dome, that protects us from the everstorm."

"Isn't that a bit half-assed help?"

His eyes narrowed. "Can you help those you love as much as you wish? What if you did your best, and the ones you loved replied that it wasn't enough?"

She winced. Did he poke at her burden so lightly? Could he know? But Vo Jie was some kid from the mines, who'd managed to stay alive longer than most. She wasn't a God. Surely that made a difference.

"Suppose he can't help us. Why aren't we doing anything to help ourselves?"

Ny Auv turned the cup in his hands. "Why are you here?"

Their eyes met, and Vo Jie glanced away. "A child," she answered. "Asking questions I can't answer. Who won't stop asking, even knowing what could result. It's riled me up, you could say. She has, or her questions have. Specifically, why are we withering away? Why are we following rules that continue our demise? Why aren't we trying to help? Priest Ny Auv, what is the core?"

"Chief Vo Jie, you could land us in grave danger."

Grave! And how did he know her title? She hadn't used it. And *grave* . . . he might as well have said death.

"Priest Ny Auv, this is my issue. We already are."

"Ny Auv." He leaned back in his chair, letting go of the cup. "Please. Just Ny Auv."

"Then, Ny Auv. Some things are growing clear to me. Not just this last day, but even these last moments."

She ignored the slight tilt to his neck.

"I will do what must be done, grave or not. And if you don't want to see me again, please tell me. Now."

He looked as if he wanted to say something, but he did not. Good enough, then. She wasn't here for games.

"I watched my brother die. It was my fault. He was too weak for the mining shift, but I had ambition to rise in ranks, hoping then I could help him. Instead, I watched him die." She pulled the locket—a relic from the old days, perhaps more precious even than the rarities in this room—from her shirt. She opened it, for only a moment. To show him.

"This is my brother's hair. He existed. He still does, to me. He was real. Why would Lord prevent me from remembering him? From learning from these mistakes, so we do not make them again. Why? Why are you and I here? Like this?" She clicked the locket closed and slid it under her wrap.

With a forceful exhale, Ny Auv rose from his seat and paced around the room. "What is it that the child said? It could not just have been that our situation is dire. Frankly,"

Vo Jie noticed a harder edge to his expression, "it would not take a scholar to assess that."

"No. It wouldn't," she agreed. "She told me that the core makes the magic. Not the mages. And please, do not spend your breath arguing it. She has used it herself. The mage, he won't say anything, but there is terror in his eyes. Distance. He is not well. None of them are well. The child, she is trying to save her brother, too. What will the magic do to her while she tries, alone, to help?"

She stood up. "Except, she is no longer alone. So. Are you a friend to us or not? I don't want to die and leave her to suffer, not because I trusted a stranger with kind eyes. So tell me now. I'm too old to play like this. What is going on?"

"I wish I knew," he raised his hands in front of him. "It's why I'm here, Vo Jie. I studied too long in the library. I asked too many questions. Bad faith, they called it. I would have received Judgment by now, if they couldn't use me here, where no one else wishes to be."

"Stop using their words," Vo Jie's frustration grew. "I see it now. They are controlling us by them, as much as by their action. They were not going to send you Judgment. They were going to kill you? Right? That's what they considered? That is Judgment?"

"I—" he seemed unable to continue.

Vo Jie had spent much of her life remembering death. She'd not imagined that for someone who'd spent their whole life avoiding thoughts of death, it might be hard to reconnect to the idea.

Ny Auv fumbled for words, finally leaning forward against the chair. His thin hands wrapped around the top bar, the skin tightening over the knobs of bone. Finally, he nodded. "I suppose so. If you leave, you are not mentioned again. I saw it before. Death, then." His face looked like he had swallowed something foul. "Death," he repeated.

His next words came out like a long exhale, and Vo Jie knew not to interrupt them.

"The mages have something to do with the upkeep of the dome," he said. "With its repair. They use the core fragment in this service. There is no furnace. The warmth filters through, as it can, from the star, from the clear moments in between the tumult of the everstorm. The outland is intemperate, unpredictable. The last trees creak and fall. The crops wither.

"I am sworn to secrecy never to discuss the core, or its need. Clan Temple says if the people learn that the dome itself falters, they will lose hope. They must think it unyielding, so we have the strength to wait until his Return. Clan Temple—our faith is strong enough to trust in Lord's design, but others may not understand. And so we protect them."

He breathed in.

"That the core fragments produce the magic; I did suspect it. All the priests do, I think. Suspect, or know, maybe. We are the only ones permitted to know that when the core is delivered to us outside the furnace, that clan Mage takes it from us into the secluded structure. One of our roles is to keep people away from that structure, for their protection. But, why else would the fragments go to clan Mage? If not in the service of magic?

"In other words, in all my years of broad access, I've only learned the facts that your child has already discovered while trapped in the dark."

Vo Jie wanted to argue, to say that he surely knew more, details, maybe that he was accustomed to, but would help them. Yet he slumped forward now, as if he had released a great burden and now looked to topple from the weakness of it. He needed time. She would not press him, today.

"I'm sorry. I don't have the answers here for you that you seek." He pulled the chair out and sat again, his head hanging.

"May we speak again?" Vo Jie was surprised at the softness of her voice.

When he looked up, his eyes were wet.

Vo Jie took it for her answer, grasped her lamp, and left.

07 Outland

Gu Non was ready to find some priests. She knew the direction outland must be—she'd seen that window after all, and you didn't forget a place like that. But finding a door turned out a lot harder; the path they'd made to all these lies sure was crooked. Memorizing each bend and full stop, she concentrated, tired from the darkness, tired from the climbing. Murmuring to herself, she repeated she hadn't come this far just to turn around.

And when she finally reached the doorway, the time and struggle it had taken to find it was erased. All she could see, now, was the light.

She'd imagined the outland to be a mirror of the mines. Some people got to live outside, and others inside. For each passage of the mines, the outland had its equivalent, shining with the light of a huge gold lamp, perhaps.

She'd not imagined this.

First, the mountainside spread around her with terrifying openness, steeply to her back and sloping to her front, its jagged edges looking like the walls of mine tunnels, turned inside out. Beyond them, rocks turned to a brown scruff, dotted with large, uneven poles of wood. And it was not a small distance—it was a vast, well, she didn't know the word for it—like the floor of a room so large it could not be described. She could walk and walk and walk, and never hit a wall.

Her eyes struggled to see so far away, and she squinted through her fingers at the shock. Yet, as she relaxed, an image formed, of wavy shapes and structures of stone rising. Like there was no such thing as close or far, just a big glowing picture.

Her eyes hurt trying to view it, so finally she looked up.

She expected to see the broad amber dome, like the ceiling of each room, but in golden shimmer, instead of the dark rock of the mines. Instead, she saw a blotchy smoke, crawling over an endless barrier with the movements of a living being. In patches, the huge rounded dome shuddered, as particles and bolts of sparks hurled against it. Only in patches, as it swirled and passed, could she catch glimpses of the shining amber behind it, which the light pushed through in thick, angled columns, where it hit the wide, brown land below.

Gu Non fell to a seat.

Her life had been measured in passages. Mark one way as correct, mark another as flawed. Determine the choices with which to sneak, pass, and learn.

How could she walk in a world with every possible passage? A world inside of one big room? Wobbling to stand, she half-stepped, half-stumbled down the mountainside, figuring if nothing else she could walk toward the shapes in the distance. There were no people here, just the tracks of the carts that carried supplies in, and core fragments out.

Just in case, she left the tracks, passing through the scruffy areas instead.

It was a long walk to the structures in the distance. Several times, she stopped to rest, including a long time where the light stopped altogether, and unsure of the way, she allowed herself to sleep, curled as best she could under a small jut of rocks.

Lord's voice still flashed in her mind, though she tried her best to ignore them. The voice never left her now. Even when it faded, some echo bounced in her thoughts. Memories she could never forget. Their need to protect overrode all else, but there was more—the darkness of it. She felt that now, as Lord's bitterness had joined those first emotions of pure protection.

Had whoever Lord was protecting been hurt? It seemed that way.

I have failed you.

"Yes, I know," she said allowing the voice some room for a moment. "If you want me to help you, I need more than that. You tried to protect someone and failed? Us? But we're still here."

Barely, though.

"I mean, we're figuring it out. I'm working on it, Lord. Trying to."

She hadn't brought food, other than one pressbar that she'd skipped a meal to save. And once that was gone, her stomach pinched, even more than usual. She found some water on the ground to fill up, so at least she wasn't thirsty as she walked.

Over time, the waves and structures grew, until the shapes of people formed in what she could see, walking, hunched between the structures, which towered over them. She didn't know what to call such a place.

What surprised her the most—for one could only really be so surprised by something they could never have imagined—was how everything here seemed to be falling apart. The walls were rough, surrounded by rings of debris, as if pieces fell from them. Without anyone to help. Just, breaking.

The oddest thing was that no one looked her way. No one really looked much at anyone, she thought. In the mines, where you were and where you were supposed to be were as important as the water and the air. Here, people acted busy, but they were minding their business. No one cared that Gu Non was here.

She relaxed, glad that uncomfortable mining cap could stay in her pocket, along with her sick tie. Walking a little taller, she continued on.

It was like all the rooms were walled off here, but not the passages. She wasn't sure how to feel about it. And there was a breeze everywhere, like when the mages were cleaning the air. But it happened all the time, and she didn't see any mages. Though, they were here, she knew.

She walked between the tall walled areas. It didn't seem very efficient to build walls around everything, but maybe with the breeze they had to. Who knew. She peered around, wondering if she should just ask directions to the Temple, or if that would set off alarm.

One structure was less broken than the others, and, she figured pretty quick, this must be the Temple. It had symbols that the priest wore, and it was painted with accents in gold. No, this was definitely it.

Gu Non felt less fear of being discovered here than she had in the mines. Here, she didn't exist. Here, her family didn't exist. If there were traps here, she couldn't possibly learn them all, not without food or supplies, so she might as well just get to why she was here.

She marched right up the stairs, proud of herself as she recognized the sigil of clan Temple. She bore no sigil, herself. Clan Mine had none. There was no use for it. The doors were triple her height and excessively decorated, but they were still doors. Heaving, she pulled one open.

"Hello?" she called. A robed man—priests were all men—stepped in front of her, wearing robes with metallic thread. Not meaning to, she smirked. Wearing something so . . . fancy. It made no sense.

"Who goes there," the man said, more stating than asking, she noted. She tried to squash her grin.

"My name is—" Now, this was a dilemma. She had to give her clan name, here of all places. And she couldn't say *Mine*. Nor would she lie. Mages were liars, but not Gu Non. "Gu Non. Rweryn." She'd said her name, then sort of followed it with a chewy sound.

"Pardon?"

She made another sound, this one a variation.

Frustrated, the man looked like he had better things to do. "Well, why are you here? Do you seek cleansing or aid?"

"Um, yes. Aid. I need to speak to a priest. It's..." she leaned forward, "*private.*"

"Mmm." From the looks of it, the man had no desire to deal with her private issue, whatever it was. Perfect. Maybe outland wasn't completely different. Gu Non was feeling pretty happy at this point. She tried to make an especially pained face, though. This person was probably a priest himself, but she wanted to do better than the guy stuck with opening the door.

Finally, she was sat down in the fanciest room she had ever seen—ha, Te Ruk's room was nothing after all—and a man asked her what he could do for her. Like the others, he looked like he had tasks to complete. Yet, a thought struck her.

"Why are priests men?"

The man looked unimpressed with the question. "In Lord's image."

"No," she said, shaking her head. "Lord is they. Not he." Truly, Lord didn't even seem to know about he or she.

The priest scrunched his face in distaste. Gu Non was just about to clarify that Lord spoke to her personally, but then suddenly realized she was being rather open here, and she'd rather have a chance of getting out on her own. Yet she didn't correct her comment. It was true, after all.

Stifling a laugh, she realized that if Lord's Book said they were *he*, then Lord must not even have written the book. But that was too much trouble to be talking about, so she continued on.

"Yes, well, I have learned some things about the core, and—"

"You should not trouble yourself with the core, child. Fuel for the furnace. Focus on Lord's protection, and faith that the everstorm will clear."

The next few minutes were no better, with the kindly man spouting the same things her own father had told her. Lord protects us. Wait for Lord. Do your part. No, she knew all that. Realizing this was going nowhere, and not thinking this was the right place to stir things up, she thanked him with many blessings, then slipped away as he tried to escort her out.

Strangely, the Temple felt familiar to her. Unlike the open whatever-it-would-be-called of the outland, the Temple had passages and rooms. Those, Gu Non understood. With the same logic in her mind, she checked each one off, figuring how to close in on the center. People kept good things in the center, usually. It's how camps were always set up.

She yanked on another huge door, gasping at what spread before her. *Books.* Books higher than rooms, well, more rooms than she could count. Books in front of her, and to her side, and suddenly she felt really mad that she couldn't read, because if she could—

"Who are you!" A robed man stomped down a curved set of stairs. Rushing to a mage tube in the wall, he called something into it.

No.

Mages she could not deal with right now. Gu Non turned and ran.

A mage, probably a woman, hastened their speed, nearly flying in front of Gu Non. Glowing blue, a wall shot out from each side, enclosing them both in a box made of mage walls.

"Who are you?"

"It doesn't matter." Gu Non suddenly wasn't sure why she had to tell anyone anything. Clan Temple or clan Mage, their rules wouldn't apply to her. She was clan Mine. Vo Jie was her Chief; she would answer to Vo Jie.

The mage sighed. "Tell me your name." In that was implied *and your clan*.

"No," Gu Non answered. "Let me go." Her temper flared at the confinement of the mage's walls, closing in on them. "Or you will regret it."

She saw the flash of light coming from the mage's hands, and without knowing what the mage could do, Gu Non reached into her pocket, pulling a fragment from the bag she'd sown of Vo Jie's scraps.

She didn't want to be here. She didn't want to face this mage, or any mage: her mission here had failed. That was something Lord understood, and Gu Non felt like a ball of light herself as she blasted through the blue wall, sped down the corridors, and shot away—not just outside of the Temple, but back up to the mountainside, stopping only when the mine entrance grew before her.

Gasping as she fell back to the ground with a hard bump, she knew what she had done was impossible. Unable to understand, she blinked, Lord's thoughts flashing in unfamiliar words, sparking in her mind in confusion and pain.

She stumbled to the door, ready to collapse, when someone wrenched their hand around her arm. Only then did she understand she was still glowing. Not just as before, but enough to light the library of the Temple.

"What have you done?" Te Ruk rasped, shaking her arm without mercy. "Where did you go? Lord! My Lord! What have you done, Gu Non? Here, we need to get you away."

Gu Non recoiled at his harsh tone, trying to remember if Te Ruk was friend or enemy. His grasp was harsh, but not cruel. She saw the terror in his eyes, reflected in the blue light.

We must protect them.

We have failed.

Bitter bitter bitter bitter bitter bitter bitter.

Nea mashak ra telkya ummbaaan.

Her legs faltered under her and she had the sensation of more blue light, as Te Ruk carried her, one passage after another, whimpering as he tripped through the passage. Just as she recognized the camps' outer ring, they collapsed together, her own blue light finally fading and Te Ruk gasping in pained cries, as he glowed himself now. "Sorry. So close. It's in me too, Gu Non. Almost there. We can—"

"Well, look who you found. What a strange surprise. Deep mission deserter? Oh, there's only one place for that."

No.

Ri Wid's cruel laugh echoed around the curved passage. Her eyes met Te Ruk's for a moment, and she didn't know what he was going to do.

He did nothing.

Cackling, Ri Wid dragged her away, but not toward their camp. Gu Non kicked and yelled, but he was larger and much stronger. And with her arms clasped in his grasp, she could not reach her pockets. She prayed to Lord that he would not search her pockets. Then, she understood.

He is taking me to controlled labor.

I failed them.

Not now, Gu Non scolded. *Not now.*

08 The Open Door

Any time Vo Jie was actually in her room, she spent it staring at the open closet door.

She wasn't there very long, because she had a clan to run. A clan that was struggling and starving, with its structure growing calloused and cruel. A clan without purpose or hope, just one unending mission that turned out to be a lie. No, Gu Non had had all of that right.

So Vo Jie could either keep working, trying to hold together the last threads of function within her world, or she could go figure out where one child had gone.

Normally, she'd grit her teeth and figure out how to do both. But an illness had taken over one of the crews, and Vo Jie had barely been able to keep up with requesting aid from outland, and quarantine, and redirecting others to move them away from what she knew to be the disposal of bodies that would never be discussed again. Her best blessing at this point was that she hadn't caught it yet. As far as she knew.

She felt sick. A different sick, she thought.

Where was little Gu Non, and how was Vo Jie supposed to choose between her well-being and potentially the well-being of all? Or worse, how could she sacrifice her own for a whim that this girl was the one who could help the rest?

Worst of all, how had she let it get to this?

She'd done the best she could. She'd tried to.

Ny Auv had been there, blessing the ill and passing orders to Te Ruk, as well as another mage who'd been called in to assist. She and the old priest acted like they'd never met, avoiding each other and staying to their business. Though, if anyone had been paying attention, they'd have seen the opposite. Their eyes watching the wall as they exchanged quips. The overuse of formal language and stunted responses.

She had the feeling the man wished he'd never met her, never heard her blasphemous talk. Well, he would have been better off that way.

Vo Jie dropped her head into her hands and stared at the table.

Gu Non had been set on visiting the priest, but she hadn't. She wasn't at her camp, not the last time Vo Jie had casually wandered past, something she couldn't do often without notice. The mines were a stale, lonely place—there just weren't many places to go.

Te Ruk hadn't seen her, not last they'd talked. It didn't help that the mage was growing incoherent; it was hard to get much from him at all. After Gu Non had pointed it out, Vo Jie couldn't believe she'd dismissed the slide for so long. She now wondered how many of the other mages were deteriorating this way, with other clans allowing it for eccentricity.

Nothing made sense here; it never had. So everything made sense, in a strange way. There was always something new to justify. It was how they survived.

The best she could figure was that Gu Non had found a place to conduct magic in secret. Some old tunnel. That could take Vo Jie forever to search, and if Gu Non was as clever as she thought, Vo Jie might never find her.

Except, she'd need to come back for food. She'd need to return to one of the sources of water. Mages couldn't create those from nothing.

Standing on tired legs and trying not to think how long the girl had gone now without food, she would at least check the child's camp one more time for clues. It had been long enough; checking their line-up as part of a standard walk-through should go unnoticed.

She recalled Gu Non's crew Boss as she walked, a truly unpleasant man. He'd had a bad past himself, one he couldn't even talk about for the death it involved. Disallowed from mourning his own family, he'd become a bully, his only joy in inflicting cruelty. A sad echo of what he could have been.

And for what. There wasn't enough space in her heart right now to defend him.

They were lining up for shift when Vo Jie arrived. At the sight of her, they quieted, rushing into position, as their Boss turned to see who approached. Vo Jie surveyed the line, and Gu Non's mother spared a moment for a long look. Vo Jie stared back, trying to read something in her expression. Something had happened. Something she knew.

"Chief Vo Jie," their Boss offered, turning to nod his eyes. "Lord's blessing."

Vo Jie left the greeting unanswered, taking to her notes. She didn't want to overplay her interest, so she started in with standard questions. Precautions against disease. Need to ration. She tapped the pages with a pencil, trying not to show extra interest. The answers held no clues.

Hoping to prick the bully's interest, she casually dropped in a line about the deep missions. It worked.

"Funny you should mention them, Chief Vo Jie." He smiled as if recalling a joke. "Remember that runt you took? For deep? She *deserted*." The cruelty in his laugh would have stung harder if Vo Jie weren't so tired. Instead it rubbed raw against the openness of her pain.

"What?" Vo Jie tapped her clipboard, as if distracted. "A deserter? I wasn't brought any."

For a moment, Ri Wid looked worried, scrunching his brows as he peered up. It didn't last. "No, no, I didn't bring her in. She's back there—" he pointed, "getting suited up for labor. Nothing you need to worry about." He cracked a grin. "Was going to send her there anyway. Just mentioning it, since you stopped in. Never good to lose a pair of hands, you know."

Vo Jie did her best to appear irritated. "We can't afford this right now. Didn't you hear what happened in 32?"

Ri Wid seemed to take the opportunity for show, as he

started to laugh, throwing a wink to Gu Non's mother, for which the meaning was unmistakable.

Vile. Vo Jie wished she didn't have such cursed options all the time. She'd have him removed, then. There'd be a whole host of cascading issues to solve, and it might put a spotlight on 71 that she didn't want, but—

Gu Non emerged from the tunnel and turned out onto the line, directly into the lamplight. A huge bruise spread across her left eye and down onto her cheek, and her lip was red in spots. Almost too heavy for her to hold, thick chains pulled down on her young arms, the metal pressing into her skin. The bright light illuminated her, casting a stark shadow on the wall behind.

By all tradition, Gu Non was a deserter. She deserved controlled labor. Likely to not come back and never be mentioned again. Yet, Gu Non had opened Vo Jie's eyes. In more ways than one. She turned to Ri Wid.

Then she stopped. Gu Non was shaking her head.

Vo Jie didn't understand. She didn't want her to go off this way. She'd suffered enough. Besides, it was clear now, whatever she was up to—they needed her. Or, more, Vo Jie could no longer imagine things staying as they were. Whatever change Gu Non offered, whatever small chance of change, it was better than this.

"Which one is she?" She asked it to stall, while she tried to sort the options. Her mind was tired, and not cooperating.

"Gu Non," Gu Non herself answered, stepping forward with a set jaw.

Ri Wid spun around and slapped her, his palm connecting right over her bruise. "Introduce properly to your Chief."

There was a long silence. Or perhaps a short silence but it felt like a million silences, as lights flickered past the child's eyes, like the reflection of a passing train of lit carts. She raised her chin.

"I am Gu Non None."

Half of the miners gasped, and by instinct, Vo Jie turned toward them. The face of Gu Non's mother was obscured, but others gaped, laughed, or recoiled. Vo Jie tried to think.

None. No clan. What had she said? It was obvious, of course. Defiance. Resolution. But . . . it wasn't. The defiance was more complex, there were thoughts flickering in Gu Non's eyes. She felt that it was . . . a message.

Her eyes met Gu Non's. Then snapped away.

Vo Jie laughed, a weak laugh, but she hoped it would suffice. "I take it back; she'll be no loss to us. But, Boss, no more punishment. They'll need her strength in labor."

She tried to send Gu Non's mother a final desperate look, but she was still facing the other side. Vo Jie had stayed too long already. She turned and walked away.

The child had not wanted her here. She tried to understand it. And she was a child. Just small. She hadn't seen the web of consequences that Vo Jie had lived, that she saw sprawling before them. Didn't Vo Jie have the obligation to intervene? Her hands shook, feeling the rusty, hard metal as if it was on her own arms.

One chance. She would give the child one chance. Tormented whether she'd decided wrong, she stumbled away, thoughts of her Gu Non now mingling with images of her brother. Her first failure. Dead.

And by the time she reached her room, she resolved it wasn't going to happen again. She'd have to go find where they'd sent her. She'd have to break her out. She'd lose all this, she knew.

That was fine. She'd never deserved it.

Then, whatever supplies she could pack. And from there, whatever happened would happen.

She'd be Vo Jie None too. Though hearing her own thought stunned her, for the child, it was worth it. For all of them.

As the door swung open in front of her, she stopped cold. A man huddled in the side of her room, shaking against the wall.

"Took her. They took her," Te Ruk murmured, his hands tucked into his robes. "Little one."

"Yes, I know," she replied, not to be rude, but her own mind felt it couldn't keep up. "Let's go get her." Yes, this was better. A mage at her side, they could find Gu Non this way.

"Not . . . I'm not sure. She . . . she's so powerful."

"Powerful?" Vo Jie offered a hand to help the man lift up, but he didn't take it. His shaking form in the corner made her uncomfortable. She'd seen a lot of pain, a lot of suffering, but weakness was forbidden here. Weakness could not be tolerated. All was done to outlast the everstorm.

Yet this powerful man, from clan Mage itself, huddled in her corner, his head turning from side to side and his eyes flickering.

"The fragments. She uses them now. Like us." He choked each word out like a stab wound, and Vo Jie understood how difficult they must have been to say. What Gu Non had said was true, then. She'd believed her already—there was a *truth* to the girl. But hearing even this much, from clan Mage. Finally, realizing he was not going to take it, she lowered her extended arm, and hobbled, weary, to a chair.

"So the fragments have power," she started, not wanting to distress the man further by reference directly. "But then, she would need fragments." And in controlled labor, they swung only, and the crew Bosses removed the fragments. A precaution that she'd never questioned.

She turned to Te Ruk. *Ah.*

"Te Ruk. I want you to listen to me. I've been helping her too. Let's both help her now. Now, why shouldn't we go try and find her? She'll need help to unclip her chains." Getting her released from them would take more coordination, but they could get her back first.

He shook his head. "No. We . . . stay. We keep our positions. She might . . . need us. She . . . has fragments now. It's why I let her go. When that creep took her."

"But," Vo Jie worried aloud, "they could take the fragments from her. Won't they search her? Remove them?"

Te Ruk started to laugh, a humorless cold laugh with a chilling edge. By instinct, she sat back in her chair, running her hands over the old, worn table's surface.

"If they would have tried to remove them from her, we'd all know by now."

Vo Jie felt every bit of fear that laced Te Ruk's laugh. "I'll trust you on one condition," she said, keeping her voice steady.

For a moment the mage looked almost cogent, as he snapped his face up to hear her terms. She'd never noticed how young the man was. It didn't matter.

"One day, Te Ruk Mage. If she's not back, we're going to get her. And you're going with me."

"It won't be a day," he said, not looking back as he stumbled out into the hall, leaving the door open behind him.

09 Chains

Ri Wid was a gross, disgusting man, and Gu Non had decided she'd do anything to get away from him. Turned out, controlled labor was a hard anything to take. She leaned over the trench and swung the pick again, cursing the weight of the metal rings that sought to pull her arms from her.

Any pain or difficulty she'd imagined shrunk in comparison to the reality of the dark place. Each miner was placed in a line along an exposed section of core, but far enough away from each other that they could not talk without the Boss hearing it. And while small lamps were shone on the core wall, in the vaster darkness around them, the others were shapes in the distance. Unknown people, whose offenses she didn't know, living what was left of their assignment— perhaps of their life—in solitude and misery.

Each swing was harder than the last, each tug of the metal more miserable. Hearing the clinking noises to her side, she wondered what it was that kept people here going. How they were able to swing one more time.

Her hands were encased in mining gloves, but these had bound fingers like a baby's sleep mitten, leaving her hands to grip the heavy tools in a clumsy pinch, like two fumbling pliers instead of a person's hands.

And while the elbow-length gloves at least kept the metal bands from rubbing her aching skin, they gathered sweat all inside them. And in chains, she couldn't fan herself, scratch what itched, or even clean the dust that gathered on her face.

Her lips stung from where Ri Wid had slammed her into the wall, more bothersome than the deeper pain that had settled into the tissue of her face. He hadn't hurt her eye, she at least thought with cold thanks.

Taking a moment in between swings, she tested whether she could reach into her pocket. She could, with some stretching, since both arms had to move together, and there was a twist involved. Yet the willpower to do it didn't worry her. Anything to get out of this place.

She gasped and fell forward as a swift kick met the back of her knee. With her arms in chains, she couldn't absorb the blow with her gloves, but not wanting to land on her knees or smack her face into the edge of the metal trench, she was at least able to turn, taking the fall with her upper arm. Sharp shards of common stone scraped her as she tried to regain balance.

"Go faster," the Boss growled. The Boss here didn't even tell them their name. Didn't need to know it, when all they were supposed to do was mine, pee, and sleep. She would add *eat*, but that blech they'd given her on the way here didn't count as food.

And so, as Gu Non struggled to her feet, then struggled to grasp and control the heavy pick with her arms heavy and fingers bound, she decided her first shift here was going to be her last.

The fragments she'd taken to the Temple were still in her pockets, minus the one she'd used to get out. She still wasn't sure what had happened, how she'd flown like a ball of light, faster than what could even have been possible. But if she could do that, she could find a way out of here. She only needed a fragment. Just enough time to reach into her pocket.

Trying not to spend all her remaining energy at once, she did need to get those eyes off of her. Whimpering as though broken, she picked away at the blue wall, loosening the core so that the Boss could later come by and collect the fragments that fell down into the metal trench against which she stood, the strange way they did it here. Truth was, that wrecked the fragments. There was no measuring here, no standards. Just the Bosses sweeping the core down the trench into metal boxes, which they locked and stacked into the carts.

Still, doing the thing that made no sense, she focused her energy into the wretched burn of her arms. She tried to pretend like each burst of pain gave her power, that she was growing huge, like a monster. Despising the way the deep trench made her awkwardly bend to get over it, Gu Non swung to loosen the core, piece by piece, until satisfied with her efforts, the Boss walked back the other way.

This was not a game she was playing for long. And the pain was starting to win.

She swung the pick. Once, twice, again, barely budging the dense wall of core.

Her arms would have screamed if they had voices. The Boss was a ways down now, and she wasn't sure how much farther they'd go. Maybe new people always got watched. So Gu Non kept silent. Stretching piece by piece, she moved her bound fingers down into her pocket, the rough chains tearing at the fabric of her tunic. While worried the Boss might turn to see her, she still didn't stop, desperately trying to pinch at one of the fragments wrapped inside.

As hard as she tried, she couldn't force her gloved hands far enough into the pocket without tearing it completely. At least then she could use the fragment, but she would need her pocket again. Her few possessions, resting in it. And the Boss had turned back, seeing she was up to something. *Need a fragment. Need a fragment.* Yet, here was a whole wall of them. She almost laughed. Lurching forward, she knocked one clear off with her pick, blocking it with her glove from falling into the trench. She dove as the hard blue stone tumbled to the ground and she encased the fragment fully into her mouth.

She let herself fall back onto the rocks, rolling onto her side as blue light streamed from her face and the Boss ran at her, shouting. One of the chains caught on the other, causing her a surge of hot pain. *Go away,* she thought. *Leave me alone.*

Gu Non was angry.

The anger burst from her in flashes of red, a searing heat that shimmered on the ground in front of her, rising up in a wall of flame and casting an orange glow over the blue wall. With a howl muted by her closed mouth, she rolled over and pressed her chains down onto the red patch of floor, watching as they weakened in the glowing mass. The heat grew against her face as, straining, she pulled the chains apart and jumped to her feet. Seeing the thick gloves starting to melt over her hands, and the pieces of chain still dangling from them, anger grew, and this time the chains burst off of her arms entirely, almost exploding as the metal pieces clattered to the stone and against the metal of the trench.

Hearing shouts and confusion behind the wall of fire, she started to rip her hands out of the gloves, but stopped. Grabbing several larger chunks she'd broken from the wall, she shoved those into her pocket until it was full, then she ripped off the gloves and threw them to the floor, right into the fire where they melted into goo. Maybe there was use for them, but she didn't care. She'd never use those foul things again.

She stumbled away, finding her way by the glow still emanating from her, as she reached into her mouth and pulled what was left of the fragment into her shaking fingers. The voices that had been shouting were not in the mines, they were inside her. She'd pushed them away, needed to get away. Now, hopefully far enough from where she'd been, she dropped to the floor, staring at her burned and blistered hands and arms, bright blue with the remainder of the fragment slowly shrinking inside it.

Anger anger anger anger anger anger anger anger anger.

She could no longer hold the voices away, and over-whelmed, she collapsed.

Betrayer!

Betrayer consumed them. Betrayer. Enemy's ally. Those were their names forever now. Enemy. Betrayer. They were ours. Ours. Enemy promised me. They promised.

Gone. Gone! Betrayer consumed what was ours. Enemy told them. Enemy told Betrayer, let Betrayer in.

There will be no forgiveness. Ever.

Anger anger anger anger anger anger anger anger anger anger anger anger anger anger.

○

It was a long time before Gu Non recovered some of her own mind, and even longer as, weak and without water, she tried to find her way back to camp. The thoughts did not fade as they had before. These thoughts were strong. They consumed her, just as Lord was furious about whatever had been consumed of theirs.

The anger inside of her flashed, hitting her just as hard as if physically punched. The fury was poison, flashing in splotches in her mind.

No forgiveness.

Lord's anger had burned the ground, it had exploded her chains, it had even seared her own weak skin, in patches where she'd been too close to the fire. Just as Lord couldn't forget what had happened, Gu Non could not either.

Yet, she didn't know what that was. What Betrayer had consumed. What Lord had tried to protect.

Wasn't Lord said to protect the Varr? Was that where they had failed?

She had realized something very important, as the two stories connected in her mind. It was Lord's anger that had burned in fire. Their rage. Fury. Gu Non could have burned the entire mine with it, had she wanted to, and had she placed her hand on the core itself, not just a fragment. Just as before, their bitterness had weakened her, drained her emotions. And before that, the barrier had surrounded her, when she'd needed to be protected. Thinking about whatever Lord had tried to protect. And failed, she now understood.

They betrayed us! You let them! You should have known!

And so she now knew, just *knew*, what the mages were hiding. It was the only thing that made sense. The mages made the dome. Lord's Dome. They used the fragments to tap into Lord's sense of protection, creating the barrier that surrounded them, covering them from the everstorm's assault. And they needed more fragments to keep generating the dome.

Whatever emotion one put into the fragment, they received Lord's emotion in return. Maybe, she even considered, the mages didn't know this. They prayed for protection, and received it. Probably much more afraid of the fragments than Gu Non had been, their minds were trained. Think only of protection. It made sense. Otherwise their world would be a madness of flames and bursts, for the power of Lord's feelings.

It was a much safer mind to think only of Lord's protection than to consider their rage. What Gu Non had touched today should have been left alone. They all should be left alone.

They are gone forever.

Maybe clan Mage knew that the fragments damaged one's mind, but they channeled still, desperate to protect the Varr as long as they could. And clan Temple, they let them—she saw it now—guided only by the greater goal of outlasting the storm. And Gu Non knew, with great sadness, her mind was damaged too. Pierced by each discovery, by the power of Lord's thoughts.

And if she was going to walk around with a damaged mind, then she was going to figure out what was going on and save Da Eel. Save Ma Mav. Save Vo Jie. Even Ri Wid, that piece of slime, would be saved by Gu Non's bravery.

She would try again, after rest. Other emotions, other pieces of the puzzle. She could do this. She could save everyone.

But now, finding familiar markings she knew would lead her back to camp, she was going to get some water, some food, and then some rest.

Betrayer consumed them. You let Betrayer in.

Enemy can never be forgiven.

10 Burn Marks

Vo Jie had accumulated more over her decades than she could fit into a bag.

This idea shamed her, thinking about it. There was no room for indulgence and collection. Not with clan Mine ill and starving, dwindled down to a point where even children were called in its service.

It wasn't just Vo Jie's forbidden necklace, a treasure beyond value, that hung from her neck. It was a hand-carved pen. A fragment of mirrored glass, polished down and fit into a wood frame. A cloth-bound notebook, painted with little flowers. A polished stone. Each told its own story. Stories Vo Jie remembered, though the voices who had told them were gone. Stories of greater value than the objects that encapsulated them.

Yet what story had she deserved when she'd watched a child punished for the simple act of trying to save her people. For the more complex act of asking questions. Seeking truth. For resisting, where Vo Jie had only complied.

Vo Jie stared at the door, closed against the passage beyond. Gu Non's time had almost run out. In one more signal, she would go find Te Ruk. And a new life, one without pens and mirrors, would begin. A life without clan.

The door slammed. Vo Jie turned to see whether it was a tunnel draft, and saw Gu Non, leaning against the inside of the door, her breath heavy. A hint of flicker filled her eyes, similar to the one she'd seen in Te Ruk's, yet punctuated with severity. What had the girl seen?

"Gu Non, Lord's blessing you've returned." Then she got a look at her.

In addition to the bruises and cuts she'd had before, there were chunks gashed from her face, and areas of burned skin. Her arms had a raw tinge to them, and some of her hair had been singed off, giving it an asymmetric look, starkly divergent from the standard cut.

"No one should be allowed to hit people," she said, still curling her fingers back against the door. "And controlled labor needs to end. It's mean."

Vo Jie wasn't ready for philosophy; the first worry on her mind was what Gu Non had done to arrive in such a state. And what she needed to do to protect her. Or maybe, protect the camps if the Bosses came for her. The mines thrived on order, not disruption. The child was too young to understand the magnitude of what she'd likely done.

"Sit down," was all she got out, ushering the trembling girl into her guest chair.

Vo Jie wished she had more to treat her wounds. Some were trained in each camp, but she couldn't call them here. Or wouldn't.

Her balm was almost out, but she sat the small tin onto the table, easing off its lid. She had a small store of vinegar, she remembered. It wasn't popular here anymore, with the amount of sickness and ill-tended digestion, so she hadn't felt so bad keeping it herself. Rummaging on her supply shelf, she brought the chipped bottle down and set it next to the balm. The stopper popped out into one hand, and Vo Jie set it to the side, pouring the gold liquid into the center of one of her bandages. She carefully pulled what was left of the balm onto a finger.

"May I?" Gu Non nodded as Vo Jie dabbed the tendable wounds, with as much care as she could. Still not sure what to say to the child who was almost a stranger but now so much more, Vo Jie could only express her emotion through gentle dabs. She hoped, compared to being struck and chained, her gesture conveyed.

"Will they be looking for you?" She kept her voice low.

Gu Non did not speak, but gave the miner's signal that they would.

Concern stabbed through her care, jarring her back to the true situation. Only one door separated them from questions she couldn't answer. From Gu Non being led away and her name forgotten. Vo Jie unable to stop them.

Setting down the cloth, she leaned her body against one of the cabinets, trying to scoot it over enough that it would prevent the door from opening. But it was full of old papers and other objects, and she could not move it alone. Understanding, Gu Non rose to help her.

Except, she gave Vo Jie a wave, shooing her away. And with a hand reached into her pocket, a faint sheen formed around her as the cabinet glid into place. Vo Jie struggled not to react.

"What do you need, Gu Non?" she asked instead. Anything. Anything she would find for her.

"Time."

The answer surprised Vo Jie, coming from a voice so young. All Vo Jie had ever had was time. And it was all she had left. Well, then. Her spirits lifted, just a tiny bit.

"We can dump wastewater there," she pointed to the side drain, not wanting to say directly that they could relieve themselves in the room. "But, no, I'll need to be out there, if we want time. Or we'll lose the room."

She stopped. Of course Gu Non understood this. The cabinet had been a calmant, but the child had obliged it. Vo Jie was still Chief. For now. What, then, could they do? "Gu Non . . . I need to know some of it. Not everything, but I can't be left in the dark, when maybe I can help you?"

Gu Non removed her hand from her pocket, and Vo Jie glanced away from an azure glow at the tip of her finger, the same color as the mage light that ran through the closet.

"I went outland," Gu Non started.

By decades of instinct and training, Vo Jie straightened, ready to chastise or punish. She stopped, stepping back.

Gu Non let her eyes land on Vo Jie for a moment only, then drew them aside. "I went outland, to talk to the priests, thinking the ones here would not be very good."

The comment stung.

"But the priests of the Temple were not helpful. It was a waste of my time. Except, there was a library there." She paused.

Then, Vo Jie recalled, they didn't teach reading anymore.

Unless one had a mentor with an heirloom book and a passion to teach rather than sleep, none of the youth read now. Even the checklists had changed to symbols.

"They caught me looking, I guess they thought I could do something with them." Gu Non's eyes narrowed. "Well, I could have. I would have found books and taken them here. One at a time if I had to." Her face drew, pressing to fury. "I escaped."

In Gu Non's brevity, Vo Jie knew there was something she wasn't saying about that escape. She hoped no one was hurt. She shuddered a bit, her eyes focusing on one of Gu Non's wounds.

Gu Non relaxed, somewhat. "It was nothing how I thought outland would be. It is perfect, in a way. Endless light and texture, and no walls except the ones that people make." She looked up. "Have you been there?"

"Yes," Vo Jie answered. She couldn't imagine how to tell Gu Non the agony of her visits, dulled over the years, but not lesser, of offering pleasing touch to those with resources, who held them just out of her reach, otherwise. Luckily Gu Non continued.

"Then you know. It's awful at the same time. They say when Lord returns, there will be only clean air and even the food will be fresh and glowing with color. The world will glow with color. I thought . . . I thought outland would be like that too. At first it was."

Her expression grew wistful, beyond her years. "Then I saw they had pain there too. Maybe less pain than here, but still. People kept their eyes to the ground, not even looking at the wonder around them. The Temple is made of metal and shine and light. But they lie there too, Vo Jie. I mean, maybe they don't all know they're lying. But they are. It made me sad."

She didn't continue, staring at the wall as if deep in thought. Vo Jie hadn't been close to children for a while, but she remembered that expression. Maybe she'd worn it herself, she thought with a pang.

"I'd like to help you, Gu Non."

She opened her mouth.

"No—don't interrupt. Not just with a room, or with time, or with anything else I can offer. I want to help you discover what else we don't understand. And if I have any chance to do that, then I need you to tell me the truth. All of it. Or—" no one should have to tell all their truth— "most of it." She extended her hand onto the table, in Gu Non's direction. "The important parts."

The ensuing silence howled with urgency to Vo Jie, who stared, still terrified, at the blocked door, but she waited, patiently, too tired and worried and too unaccustomed to conversation to make a better case for herself. She hoped it had been enough.

"The magic is somehow tied to Lord," she said, staring down at Vo Jie's hand. "The fragments allow it, when people touch them. I think . . . maybe anyone can do it. But it's really hard, too. Lord speaks in your mind. Telling a story that upsets them."

Them? She didn't interrupt.

"The mages try not to listen to the story, I think. They

use Lord to make the dome. It protects us. *Oh.*" Her head jerked, though she didn't look up. "Clan Mage makes the dome now. Not Lord. I don't know what Lord is doing, but they're not making the dome. I just . . . know that. Don't ask me, please."

Gu Non shifted. "Anyway. The mages avoid Lord's story, because they are struggling to keep going. I'm not struggling to keep going. I'm set to get out. Get us all out. And so I listen. I think maybe that's a difference. So, anyway, Lord had something that was really important to them. Some resource that they and Enemy had agreed to protect. Like, a powerful treasure. And Enemy was going to protect that with them. Um, that's what they call that one. Enemy. And Enemy had a friend or something, Betrayer, who consumed the treasure that Lord wanted to save. I'm pretty sure the important thing is gone now.

"And Lord, they were so mad about it that they promised that Enemy would never, ever be forgiven. And I need to figure out more and I'm not sure how the everstorm fits in, except it makes sense that it does, cause like, they're all pissed so someone is making it."

She paused for breath, finally almost meeting Vo Jie's eyes. She glanced back down.

"And you need time, what, to learn the story?"

Gu Non signed again, agreeing. Then she added, out loud, "I really need some water. And I think I need some rest now too."

Hearing her talk casually about Lord like a fill-in crewmate, Vo Jie had almost forgotten the age of the child before her. That she hadn't had water. Or likely food. She was hurt, scared, alone.

She was not alone.

"I have food and water. I'll make it for you. Wash off." She gestured toward her own napkin, not sure whether Gu Non still had one. "Try not to think about it all. Just for a while?" Gu Non didn't answer, nor did she argue.

"One last question." She disliked to press her, but she needed to know. "How did you escape your chains?"

"I burned them," she answered, as though the question were simple. "With rage."

Vo Jie poured the water first, and she took it, emptying it almost at once. And when she turned to see what food she could possibly add comfort to, she looked back again, and Gu Non was asleep. Fashioning her bed as best she could, Vo Jie eventually brought the food in and left it at her side.

Awkwardly, she reached a hand down toward the little face, framed by dirt and burn marks. She hadn't washed off, after all. Vo Jie's hand hovered just over her face, as though to caress her. Instead, she drew back, closed the door, and let her sleep.

11 Time Alone

Gu Non stared at the core fragment for a while. As eager as she was to move on, she was finally admitting to herself that something was happening to her. She'd thought it before, of course, but some of that was tough talk. When one really considered, really considered, losing parts of their mind, it was a little harder to be brave.

And though she'd learned new things, though she'd been new places, she hadn't helped anyone yet. Only hurt. How far could she push with this until everyone was hurt, and nothing good had been done?

Maybe there was a reason no one else had tried to change things.

Maybe the whole mine was too much to try and push.

Everyone was in trouble now because of her. Vo Jie jumped at every distant noise, and there were always noises in the mines. Te Ruk had been by once, with more fragments, and she'd barely been able to speak with him, the way he avoided her eyes and made no sense at all. She wasn't even mad at him anymore for lying—she felt bad she'd dragged him into this, when she now understood, he was part of the mine, too. Forget clan Mage. He was here, suffering with them, he was clan Mine to her now.

She couldn't shake the memory of her mother's face as Gu Non had left the camp in chains. But she couldn't risk doing anything there; she didn't know what could happen. Her mother wasn't sad or anything, she was too old and tired for sad. But she'd kept her gaze away, as if not letting Gu Non back in. Like she'd played too long in the tunnel, or something. And now she wasn't one of them. Gu Non had tried to show her she was brave, but it wasn't enough. She wished Ma Mav could understand.

And, of course, she worried about Da Eel the most. It wasn't many more shifts before he was scheduled to be commissioned. Before he'd be stuck in the tunnels, making sure his fragments were at least four ticks and surely being hit all the time by Ri Wid for problems that turd-Boss made up in his mind. Problems just meant to punish Gu Non and her Ma Mav. Because he didn't like them saying no.

It wasn't going to stop Gu Non from saying no, but it didn't make her thoughts less awful imagining little Da Eel suffering.

Another thought pulled at her. She tried to ignore it, but it kept coming back. What if Gu Non being taken to controlled labor gave Ri Wid an excuse to bring in Da Eel early? She'd already been gone, but all he needed was an excuse. Da Eel couldn't take it there, actually mining all shift, over and over. His mind was bigger than all of theirs, in its own way, but it wasn't built for mining rocks all day. Even blue magic rocks. Especially blue magic rocks.

Gu Non gritted her teeth. She grabbed a core fragment. She hadn't been sure what emotion to try next, except the emotion came to her. It was already in her. One that never asks permission. A real turd of an emotion.

Desperation.

Her hand glowed blue, and there was no need to focus on the idea. Desperation wrapped around her, swirling her in blue muck and tightness and she couldn't get herself to breathe.

Get off of me!

Surprised, she realized the images in her mind were not vague approximations of a god, but images of her own people. Regular people. The Varr. She could see them, but in a strange place. Not in the mines.

She couldn't recognize the place where they stood, walked, and ran. It was like the outland, but brighter. There were rivers of water, and the land rose and fell. The star burned bright, not like the glow outside of Lord's Dome, but a shining light, like a bright lamp that required a girl to shield her eyes.

Giant plants dotted the fields. She thought they were plants. They were huge, as large as the structures around them, with long, well, legs, she supposed. And smaller plants too. They didn't seem to be farms for food, they were just growing. There were other things moving, as well, things with eyes and faces. Not the Varr but other things, strangely formed beings that amazed her as much as they startled her.

Over time, she saw the land change. Huge, rounded beams of wood would roll from the hills, and her people would run to stop them, heaving with ropes and chains, and taking grave injuries as they pulled them away, to protect their strange outland structures.

Why did wood roll from the hills?

Water filled valleys, more water than Gu Non could imagine, and the people struggled to stay afloat, to find a place to rest.

Other times, the wind blew, and sparks cracked, like smaller versions of the everstorm.

Whatever this place was, life was not easier then. It was harder, maybe even than the mines. Gu Non's desperation grew. Would she lead them away from their suffering just to suffer more? Why must people hurt so?

Care for them.

We must hide for now.

Here. Drink. Drink it in.

I do not like Enemy's idea, and I won't do it. I don't care what we do. I don't care.

We must protect them.

Her mind was tiring quickly, and, not knowing how long she could hold the vision, Gu Non was annoyed that Lord's voice was interrupting it. She didn't understand what she was seeing, and here instead of answering her questions, they were rambling on again. And it didn't help that she was immersed in a pool of desperation herself. She didn't know why she was here. Why she'd used the fragments. Why she'd hurt her own mind, trying to help. None of it mattered, she never should have begun.

No.

Enough of herself remained to know she was feeling a

lie. That hope had not disappeared, that it was an emotion inside her. There was no hope here in this vision either. Just trials. And pools. And sadness.

Hope was an enemy here, too. Was that what Lord meant? No, their anger toward Enemy was too personal for a metaphor. Enemy was someone.

Enemy brought in Betrayer! Betrayer had no place here!

I know, I know, Lord, but what did they betray?

They consumed them.

Yes, you've told me. The connection disappeared, and again Gu Non was seeing the Varr, in this bright world made of light and color. Someone was running to another person. They cried and hugged as if they hadn't seen each other in a long time.

Drink more. Drink.

Be strong.

Then, Enemy will understand. Enemy will see for themself.

A vague thought popped in and out again of view. Enemy was not called that then. Lord's fury at their betrayal had tainted even old memory. Whatever Enemy had been before, they were Enemy now.

In the distance, she saw a towering structure, with slanted edges and sharp peaks. The Temple. Instead of damaged and worn, it stood tall above the other structures. And the star's light illuminated it, not the amber light that filtered through holes in the dome, but a pure, clean light that glistened and reflected and shone as if the world would never run out of light.

People, her people, waited in long lines to its outside,

many weeping, others with jaws set. Gu Non tried to turn away, to see what her own mountain—what the mines looked like then—but she could not. The Temple drew her, so strong, like the smell of new cooking in the central camp.

Then this was the outland, the outland before the dome. Even their happiness was sad here. It came from the relief of pain, not from joy.

Was this world—was it what she wanted to return?

You are safe, here. We are far away. I will not consume you. Just drink. Drink more.

Star's light shone in her eyes. Plants thrived and grew, and the other creatures, the non-Varr, leapt and bounded through them.

Gu Non felt she was moving too far into the vision world. Just as Lord's thoughts were memories, she knew this land was memory too. The everstorm had assaulted it, bringing even greater trials than those faced by these Varr. And Lord had made a dome of magic, to protect their chosen people, the Varr, from its continued assault.

But—Lord must be here, in this world too. They must have these memories, or Gu Non couldn't see them. Lord had allowed this. They had always allowed pain. The everstorm was just part of a greater story. The dome.

Had Lord even created the dome? The mages made the dome, right? Or was it Lord?

Black soot flew through the sky, balls of sparks and bolts of things that Gu Non could not understand. They flew at the land. The non-Varr who could, ran and ran away. And the Varr screamed. They died. She saw people die! She saw her people die! Their bodies lay broken across fields now charred by the barrage of dark and light and horrible.

Curse you, Enemy! Curse you forever. You took them but you cannot take these too.

An amber dome shot up over the land. Not all the land, but the structures and the river. She still couldn't see the mountain. As it rippled over the battered buildings and the charred land, the people screamed and ran, and the chunks of everstorm ceased falling to the ground.

They fell, with even greater fury now, but they crashed against the dome. One after the other. Familiar now, she recognized the darkening sky, the constant rumble of the everstorm against Lord's Dome.

Behind her was a crash so huge that her ears stopped working for a long moment, replaced by a terrifying ring that filled her mind, and she fell forward onto the land, no, onto the closet floor—she wasn't sure—as the crash reverberated again and again, without end.

She looked up, and the dome was no longer solid. It weakened in spots. But if it weakened, then they would all die. Die like the bodies spread throughout the city. She saw them, she stepped over them. They had always suffered, but now, death. So much death.

We have to find a way to fix it.

What is that?

Stifling a scream, she fumbled in a haze, trying to open the door. She couldn't tell anymore what was in the room, what was in the bright outland place, or what was in Lord's mind. She scraped and felt the wood of the door, unable to understand how it would open. Then it did open, and she fell forward, falling into thin, kind arms.

"Gu Non," a voice said from a very far distance. It was not Lord.

"Gu Non," it repeated. Now, Gu Non was seated.

"You are safe with me. I will take care of you." The voice was Vo Jie's. Water was set in front of her.

"Drink," she said. "Drink."

Drink!

She screamed, knocking over the water, which splashed on her legs. The metal cup rolled, and Vo Jie caught it.

"Then sit still. Whatever it is, no more magic for now. This needs to pass."

A thought had been bouncing in Gu Non's mind for a while. She didn't know how to express it, but it flittered around like a dream wisp, straining to break through all the clutter in Gu Non's frantic mind. Like a toddler, seeking attention. But Gu Non was distracted, there were too many more important things at work.

Tapping at her, the wisp would not leave, until she understood what it was trying to tell her.

Her eyes unfocused, but the shape of Vo Jie still hovering in front of her, she whispered the message that had been trying to reach her. The only words she could get out.

"I need help," she said.

Vo Jie paused. "Can you walk?" she asked. "Hurry, let's go. Now."

Gu Non fought the haze to force her legs to rise. She

followed where the wrinkled hand led her. And as they walked down the stone halls of clan Mine, her Chief said one more thing, one that she heard, quite clearly.

"We weren't safe there anyway."

12 The Power

This time, Ny Auv's door was closed. At least glad that the area was still empty, she rapped on the door, wincing at the sharpness of the wood against the thin skin of her fingers. She rubbed them, cognizant of the bumps and wrinkles. Time had a way of making its presence known through hands, more than anything else. Or maybe hands were just always in one's view. The door started to open, and Vo Jie stepped back.

Instead of the blank face he'd held at the camps, Ny Auv's expression was a whole pot of emotions, mixing together as he peeked around the opening door like a child. She'd grown skilled at reading expressions over the years of managing her clan, but this was too much of a puzzle. Unhappy to see her, happy, worried . . . she had no idea. Maybe all of it. She pointed to Gu Non, making sure he saw her there.

"Ah," he said, widening the door to let them both in.

Gu Non hadn't spoken, nor did she now, as Ny Auv led her to the long couch and helped her lie down. Blankly, she stared up at the room's ceiling, as the priest turned back to face Vo Jie.

"Then this is she?"

While Vo Jie didn't like talking about Gu Non as if she weren't there, it certainly didn't appear that she was listening. Now, with her eyes slowly closing, she couldn't blame Ny Auv much for treating her like a sleeping child.

"Yes. Look—" Vo Jie was well-tuned to the sensitivities of what could and couldn't be said, but she'd been too open with the man once, and she was still around to talk about it. She wasn't here for some drawn-out exchange.

"Don't worry." Ny Auv seemed to answer the question anyway. "My word whatever we discuss stays here. I . . . I will believe you. Or try my best, anyway."

She warmed at the clarification, as much as his offer. Sitting on a padded chair, one that looked very old but hadn't been used much by the poof of dust that her sitting stirred, she tried to think where to start.

"It is a relief," was all she said, "to not worry about hiding the truth."

He didn't seem to know what to say to that, so she began.

"The core does grant the magic. I've seen her use it. There is no need to be a mage. In fact, I've—" She didn't want to implicate Te Ruk, but she'd had the priest's word for confidence. She wanted to trust it. "I've talked to our mage, and he admits it's true. There is no magic in him if he's not in direct contact with the core. Or any piece of it."

Not wanting to be distracted or interrupted by what must be expressions of shock or incredulity, she stared at Gu Non's char-stained boots and continued to tell what she knew.

"She's been trying it. Using the magic. She's convinced we can't go on this way. That something needs to change. And her brother, I think I mentioned this, he's due to be commissioned. Neurodivergent, the little one. Charming and brilliant, but I agree he's not capable of that type of job, physical or mental. They tried to grab him already, actually, but I threw him in a closed quarantine. I can't buy much more time that way, but I couldn't pass by whatever tools I had to buy him time. And her." She nodded toward Gu Non.

"Is that all?" he asked. She could tell by his tone it was meant to be humor.

"No. There's more." She was still staring at Gu Non's burnt shoes. "When she uses the magic, she hears a voice. Or . . . maybe it is a split mind, and she can speak as well as listen within it. I don't know. But through this state, she is learning a story."

"A story," he repeated.

"It regards Lord, Lord's Dome, and the everstorm. She is learning the story in pieces, and she is convinced to complete it, thinking it holds clues to understanding the dome, or the everstorm, or, I don't know, how to call Lord back, even. Something that we need."

"And you've allowed this? You've allowed this child to play with magic."

"She's not playing. And I don't think I could have stopped her."

Her own words irritated her. Realizing why, she finally looked at Ny Auv directly. "No. I'm making excuses again. I don't *want* to stop her. I believe her. I believe she is somehow connecting to Lord, now or in a memory Lord left for us. I believe her that we cannot go on this way, whether or not her brother fuels that passion. And I believe, even if her brother were not here, it wouldn't stop her. She would save us all, any way that she could. And I'm a little embarrassed that for all the rest of our great intentions, we could not reach so far."

From the couch, Gu Non stirred.

Vo Jie gestured toward her, unable to take her eyes from the man's. "She reached too far this time. I let her alone, as she wanted, and she emerged glowing in blue and with far away sights in her eyes. I tried to talk to her, but all I could get is that she's asked for help. I can help her, perhaps. But—"

"Maybe you just wanted to see me again?"

Given the seriousness of the situation, the joke fell flat. Or, Vo Jie realized, it wasn't a joke. Their eyes connected, and she felt a longing stir inside her, one that could not be pushed away or dismissed. Her heart pressed in her chest, and she felt very far away from the man, alone in the dusty chair.

"Working together, maybe we can help the girl," she said. "That seems the most important issue right now."

"There can be more than one important issue at a time."

The silence was heavy, and Vo Jie only imagined where this might have led if Gu Non was not placed between them. Or, she was specifically imagining where it would lead.

As if needing some connection, he reached across and

placed a hand on her arm. She winced; he could not have known about her wound.

"I'm sorry," he said, alarm in his eyes. "I shouldn't have. It's just that—"

"No, stop. It's not you. I have a wound on that side. Just a small one; I keep it treated."

"A wound? How long?"

"Long enough." Whatever connection they were feeling, she didn't have to empty her own files straight away.

"I'm sorry." He stood, wincing. "I need to stop apologizing."

"I wish you would," she agreed, trying to distract herself from the pain in her arm. As the priest gazed up toward the ceiling, she discreetly tugged at her sleeve, hoping to pull the bandage up away again. It didn't quite work.

"What do you know of Lord?"

He turned with a sharp look.

"Not just you. But all of you. Clan Temple. You see, I was born clan Mine. I've always been clan Mine, and I've always been told I was clan Mine. I've spent decades dedicating my waking thoughts to ensuring the furnace was fed. You can imagine the pit that I've been trying not to fall into upon realizing there is no furnace. So, for you, Ny Auv Temple, what do you know of Lord?"

"It is different in clan Temple," he said, his voice lowering. "Clan Mine requires the most hands available. If one is born here, they stay here. If they are ill-equipped elsewhere, they are moved here. If they can't make it here, they die here."

Vo Jie stifled her gasp, allowing the man his own rebellion.

Still, he no longer met her eyes and his face flushed. It was the cutest blasphemy she'd ever seen, she couldn't help think.

"Clan Temple requires few members. Just enough to ensure the passage of secrets, enough to guard the knowledge, and enough to manage clan Mage. So those with reasons to leave never need admit them, they just offer their services to a labor clan, like Mine, Farm, or Repair. So in some ways, we are born knowing there is a choice. Even if a small, unpleasant one."

"Why did you choose to stay?"

By the cut of his eyes, there were other reasons he wasn't going to tell. "Knowledge," he answered. "I thought, perhaps by studying, I could do more to help. But they don't allow us much time there, not when there are assignments and trivia. Not to mention a long line of counseling, which I'd appreciate more if we weren't required to read from the script. See, that was my problem."

Vo Jie raised her brows.

"I can't behave and simply read from the script. Never could. Spent too much time in the library, I suppose. I said the wrong thing to the wrong person, and suddenly I'm off on mine assignment. Frankly, I think they hoped I'd never return." He glanced around. "I know it's hard to believe here, sitting here in the nicest room you have, but this place can be too much for us. We're not as strong as you."

"That's them telling you that," she muttered, feeling weary again. "Listen. There's more, and I need to tell you, in case you want to send us back out."

"I won't send you out."

"Wait and hear it," she said, almost laughing. "She snuck out to the Temple." Yes, that got his attention. "She escaped using magic. Which they likely saw. Then she was caught coming back by her previous crew Boss, who I'm sure had checked the departing deep crew and saw she wasn't on it. He threw her in what we call controlled labor, which if you haven't heard of it, you won't want to. It's just punishment to keep order."

"Hmm," he said, apprizing Gu Non's charred clothes and battered skin.

Well, yes, he'd have to be most unobservant not to have noticed all that. And the fact that she was clan Chief and hadn't ended controlled labor brought her a new sickness she couldn't yet voice. She'd never thought she could. That was no excuse, she now realized.

"I don't feel safe in my room anymore," she continued. "She's been using magic there. Our mage knows she's there, and he's weak and unstable. And I've been linked to the girl myself. Just too much chance they'll come to look. And . . . I can't leave her anymore. To go back to shift. Which means without an elaborate cover which I'm not keen to leave in order to orchestrate, I've effectively stepped down from my job."

Though light in tone, she knew it was clear to them both what she was suggesting. She rose from the chair.

"Does Lord watch over us, my priest?" There was no sarcasm in the question. Her confusion ran deep.

"I don't know," he answered. "He has spoken to the child." He hesitated. "Her name? Did you say it?"

"Gu Non," she answered. Then, breaking into a painful smile. "Gu Non None. And Lord is they, not he. She insists on it."

"Alright. Then, they speak to clan None. But they have not spoken to me, clan Temple." He started to pace around the room. "Ironically, our main job in clan Temple—I don't know if they tell you this—is to maintain faith. In Lord, in his—sorry, in their Return."

"Because if we didn't believe Lord would return to save us, why would we continue to live this way?"

He nodded.

"I don't like it," she said. She wanted to say more. She was thinking more. How much had they not considered for being told the way things were? For believing it. But it was too dangerous to say, even here, and so she bit her lip. Maybe she'd said enough.

"Our other job is to manage clan Mage. We are like . . . two pieces of a key. We direct them, with the knowledge we have. With some that I believe only our own Bosses and Chief have. They hold the tools. We hold knowledge."

"That way the power is split," she murmured. "Have you ever considered that our entire structure is based around keeping power in check? Around keeping any one person from seeing too much of the puzzle?"

They looked down at Gu Non, tossing as if in a bad dream. Vo Jie rested a hand on her shoulder, hoping it brought some comfort.

"Except this one," he said. "She is seeing more and look what it is doing to her."

"That is because we've made her work alone. Few burdens can be borne by one alone."

The mention of being alone shot a silence through the room. He was close to her now, and, there they stood, only ticks apart. Vo Jie's longing caught in her throat.

"Can we talk about it?" he asked.

"We can do more than that," Vo Jie replied. "If you'd like to."

The pressure of his lips against her own answered that question for her.

13 Hunger Grows

She must have stayed in a sense of the vision because she imagined herself on the most cushiony bed she could ever imagine. The land of the gods. The land of the gods still smelled mostly like the mine.

Gu Non was still in the mine. What was this place?

She wasn't sure. Stumbling away, she knew she was still in the active area, because the lamps were lit and the mage pipes running. Gu Non thought she knew every corner of the active area, but she didn't know these halls.

Then, this was where the assigned priest stayed. The clan Temple section. Was she in trouble here? If he'd captured her, she wasn't bound by chains or any other ties. Unsure, she wandered on, feeling her feet in the regular mine world but other bits of her still in the vision. The world with no dome.

Drink.

Why wasn't the domeless world happy? There would always be pain. Ma Mav had told her that. But she had a sense the trials of the Varr had not begun with the dome; they had only changed.

Yet, that made sense. Lord did make the dome. She knew that now. Perhaps she shouldn't have been so quick to think about whether which story was true, when both stories could have truth. A good lesson. Yes, she would remember that.

They betrayed me!

Lord made the dome, but then they couldn't protect it. Right, because they left. They left to avoid the everstorm, they protected the Varr with the dome, and then somehow, clan Mage figured out how to use the magic to repair it.

Lights. Stone. Crashing. *Crashing!* She gripped the wall, breathing heavily against the rock, a cool moss brushing her aching cheek. Slowly, she understood the crashing was not here, but in her mind.

She just wanted to feel normal again. Life had been hard, but it also had been fun. She didn't want to leave it all; she just wanted to fix it. Didn't anyone understand that? She missed Da Eel and Ma Mav. Her big siblings, playing games with them. She missed her friends.

Friends. Gu Non was going to find her friend.

Stumbling toward the camp, flashes of colorful plants and bright light confused her, but ingrained memories of the tunnel structure bubbled through it, providing her a path back to the camp. She'd lost track of shifts. Maybe they were out. No, there was sound coming from camp. They were here. Ba Dos would be here.

Making their secret whistle, she stayed over by the dark wall, the empty storage nooks for extra supplies that now never came.

He rushed over, grabbing her arm. "Gu Non. Are you kidding me? I had—"

He'd forgotten her. Not really, of course. But he thought she was dead, and so he'd put her from his mind. That made Gu Non mad. A piece of her started to return.

"I'm here. I'm here."

"But you went to controlled labor! Ri Wid bragged about it all first shift. Then, next shift, he didn't mention you at all. We all thought—"

"Oh, that," Gu Non said. "I escaped."

"You what? Smoggy bottoms, Gu Non, you can't escape controlled labor."

She actually giggled. Literally anyone could escape it, all they would have had to do was grab a fragment with their teeth. "Just eat some core fragment," she could have said. But he wasn't ready for that. Ba Dos was always a little slow to accept things. But he was bold too. She was so happy to see him, she almost hugged him right there.

Even with her mind confused, hugging friends might be too much.

Then, as her eyes adjusted to the dark corner, she saw the unease in his. "What is it?"

"I'm sorry, I just was really surprised to see you. And your hair! But, what will happen if you're back? If I don't, you know, go turn you in? I don't want to be in chains. I wouldn't know how to escape them. I think we're in danger if you're here. I'm sorry." He glanced back toward the camp.

Guilt twisted his mouth, but she actually appreciated him being honest right now. He'd always been honest. And that meant she was really here with her friend, not lost in

Lord's places. Talking with a familiar voice was calming her, bringing back pieces of her own mind. But maybe he was right. Had she endangered the whole camp by showing up in it? She hadn't thought this through; she was just confused and went walking. Maybe she should go. Friendly or not, she'd go find out why this priest had taken her. And where was Vo Jie? Well, she wouldn't be here, at just this one camp. She was Chief, after all.

"I'm sorry, I didn't mean to scare you. I'm trying to help, and I've had a lot of things happen, and I just . . . wanted to say hi. I've missed you. I can go now."

He leaned in. "I . . . I missed you too. Adults are boring, anyway. But . . . can you tell me what you're trying to do? I mean . . . do I want to know?"

"How do I know what you want to know, silly? But sure, why not. I'm using the magic to release us from the mine." She grinned.

"What?"

Men howled in agony in front of her. Kneeling down onto the soft green blades, they pounded their fists against the ground. "Why have you done this to us, Lord? What have we done to deserve such pain?"

The blaspheming men were not here, she remembered. Ba Dos was here. He leaned back, fear growing in his face.

"Lord protects us!" That was not Ba Dos. It was someone else. She straightened up and shook her own shoulders. "I'm having some problems, ok? But I want you to trust me. I'm working on things. I want to fix the mines."

"Did you say you joined clan Mage?"

"What? Oh! No. They have nothing to do with this."
Well, Te Ruk was part of it, but only because she'd trapped
him into it. That didn't count. "I'm just off on my own."

"*Wow*. The worst part is, I believe you. Bad air,
Gu Non." He stepped back. "You always were the bravest."
He paused. "I don't think you should stay here. Wherever
you were hiding, maybe you should go back there. Do you,
uh, need anything?"

She needed a lot of things, and almost snapped "my
mind back." She needed food. She needed rest. She needed
people to be able to choose a better life, and not work all
day to feed a fake furnace. Ba Dos' warm smile, though,
that made her happy.

"What I needed for now, I already got, thank you. But
what about you? How are things going?"

He didn't answer. She looked out across the camp, seeing
what she already knew. Gaunt faces. Tattered clothes.
People not even playing games anymore, but just staring at
the wall, as if willing the time to pass.

Why did you trust them?

The man collapsed before her on the grass.

She was back in the camp.

Her mind twitched, and all the logic about hiding
and keeping secrets seemed very far away. "Ba Dos, you
don't have to tell them we talked, but I want to tell you
something."

"What is it?" he asked.

"The things we think are so important not to do are not
very important at all when you get away from them a bit."

Ba Dos seemed to be thinking about it. Well, maybe he'd think some more. It was time for her to go, before she got them in any trouble.

"Gu Non?"

She turned back.

"Lord be with you."

Now that was just funny. And it gave her an idea, too. Why was she sneaking around in slightly trouble when she could be in all trouble? If the only difference was what she could do?

Walking right into the middle of the camp, she stopped. "Um, hi. You know me. So, uh, I'm doing ok. Let me see." She scanned the silent room, trying to think what she could do. She knew protection, that came to her easy now. But she couldn't just give them a bubble.

Te Ruk cleaned the water, he cleaned the air. If he could do that, she could do better.

She didn't want to show them the core fragment; that might endanger them, and she needed more time to think about if that was a good idea. So, turning real quick, she lifted her tunic and unwrapped a fragment from her pocket. She shoved it down into her pants, and turned back, glad the glow seemed to be staying inside. Now, then. Protection. Oh, and what had Lord been doing. Feeding?

Oh, now she could feel a lot. The food stores were dried and some were spoiled; she waved the magic through them, the dried fruits plumping back to fresh, and the grains rid of yuck. She freshened the water in the tubs—way better than Te Ruk did it, she gloated—and cleared the air. Oh! Sickness!

There were illnesses, here, both passing and deep-set, and, throwing a bubble around herself in case anyone got funny about it, she pulled them out, discarding them down the side drain as her friends and family gasped for air. She cleaned their clothes, their napkins.

As the commotion grew, she remembered how many people were still back in their rooms, not in the common area. Her family, they weren't here. She wanted to help Da Eel, too. And the others, even the ones who thought she was weird. She loved them too. All of them. But, she only had so many fragments, and if she ran out here, they really could end her.

Death. Yeah, she thought of it. They could kill her.

Her mind jolted, images of the bodies filling the dome as it spread across the outland structures.

Oh, death was real. And Enemy had caused it. People could cause it.

Death wasn't fiction. Death was the opposite of fiction.

Hiding death was the lie.

The calling intensified, and Ri Wid was there, smacking some long object at her that just bounced against her bubble. Others ran and others watched. And suddenly Te Ruk was there too, shouting in her direction. A blue glow blasted from him, and he joined her in the bubble.

"They aren't ready. They won't side with you yet, Gu Non. They're too scared, too trained. Where were you staying?"

She wasn't done helping yet. She still had some core.

He shook her. "Where were you staying?"

"The priest's," she whispered, hoping she hadn't just made a terrible mistake.

"Can you trust me? Please?"

She wasn't sure. Her fragment was fading and Te Ruk held her arms. He was stronger than she was, and she couldn't reach for another. He'd helped her, she remembered. She looked into his eyes.

"Double cross me and I'll wreck you," she said.

She was surprised to see his grim smile. "I wouldn't dare." Then he turned to the room, fury in his voice.

"I declare this child under the direct punishment of clan Mage. *You will not mention her again.*"

The room fell to silence, even Ri Wid, whose grin grew broad. And they stayed silent as Te Ruk led her from the room. She turned back as they crossed the doorway.

"Hey, everyone, it was good to see you. Check all the food crates—some of it's way better now."

As he pulled her back into the passage, he let go of her arm. "Just follow me," he said. "Please don't argue right now. I'm tired. And we'll need new plans."

The visions were still flashing, but with magic still pounding in her blood, she was able to stay in this world just a little longer. "I just want to know one thing," she said. "If all of us want this to be better, why do I still have to hide?"

14 Waiting to be Remembered

"What a naïve question," Vo Jie lectured, reminding herself that the mage was young, too. Though, with both of them sitting on Ny Auv's couch surrounded by a faint blue glow, maybe she shouldn't be distinguishing only one as the mage.

Of course other people had argued with the way things were. And they'd been sent to controlled labor and then disappeared. Anyone with an inclination to join them saw that pretty quickly and thought they wouldn't be much help if they weren't around. So they resigned to help in smaller ways.

Vo Jie kept the rest of it to herself. The girl's naïveité to what couldn't be done was probably the reason she'd gone this far with it. Why discourage her now.

She regretted not having kept a closer eye on the girl, but, then, she'd been under clan Mine's care her whole life, and what had that ever done for her? She seemed to have done just fine on her own. At this point, Vo Jie wasn't going to waste her remaining energy worrying about the past.

That recent decision had changed her outlook considerably.

"Well, that was it," Te Ruk finished, with Vo Jie glad

they hadn't pressed on her last remark. "She actually listened to me, and we arrived here."

Gu Non, who'd been silent, snapped into coherence. "I actually listened? I've been listening all my life, you turd-heart. Stop talking like I'm the silly little child when all of this was my idea in the first place. If you don't like it, go back." She glared at the others.

Vo Jie couldn't prevent a smile, which didn't fade when her eyes met Ny Auv's. He shrugged, grinning back.

"Gu Non," he said in a gentle voice. "You're right, of course. But we're in a bit of a difficulty. You've been seen doing magic. You've been seen, released from controlled labor after they'd ended your name. Maybe your Boss can silence that. Maybe he can't. We can hide here in this room, but we'll soon be found. We can plan here. We can storm the mine, hoping enough join us. Either way, we're a small force compared to those outland. Even in their current state, I assure you, there is more than enough power out there to ensure your voice is stopped."

She tapped her chin. "Be quiet, please. I'm trying to think."

Vo Jie exchanged a nervous glance with Ny Auv.

"But they need us," she continued. "Need clan Mine. They can't, you know, punish all of us or who will mine the core? And they need the core for the dome."

Vo Jie admired the room's lack of reaction to that statement, that could not be made less jarring by the casual way that Gu Non threw it.

Ny Auv answered her. "Perhaps you're right. But

compared to full chaos, they may risk it. A new clan Mine would form, with some from before. Those they were sure had not heard your words or those who would never consider them. Are you willing to risk the others quite yet, not knowing for sure?"

"Hmm, I don't know," she answered. "So I can just keep using fragments, hoping to learn the rest of the story. But there's two problems there. First, those fragments are getting to me. I'm not stopping, of course, but if I go too fast, I'm not sure there will be enough of me left to help."

By the dark tone of her voice, Vo Jie realized with a jump that the girl fully intended to sacrifice herself for the others, she just didn't want to burn out while she could still help. Like maximizing lamp oil, she thought with revulsion.

"The second reason," Gu Non continued, not noticing Vo Jie's reaction, "is that I just thought about something. If everything I'm seeing is from Lord's memories, then how do I know Lord's telling me the truth? Or even that they remember it all the right way."

Lord's Return, did she just say that?

As shaken as she felt, she was surprised to notice that Te Ruk looked entirely absorbed, and Ny Auv wasn't a bit rattled. He leaned forward, and began to ask her what she'd like to do.

"So there were a lot of books in the Temple," she stated. "First, I can't read. Second, I wouldn't know where to start. So, Ny Auv Temple, I guess I'm asking for your help."

Certainly he wasn't going to just—

"I will follow you to the everstorm," he said, without a

tick of drama to his tone. He glanced at Vo Jie with a hint of apology, but didn't correct his statement. "And with a high chance someone might be out making sure you actually disappear this time," he winced at his own words, but again, didn't rescind them, "I'd say we go now. Or soon," he corrected. "Once you are ready."

While Gu Non nodded at him, Te Ruk was staring at her face. "You healed the others," he said. "I saw it. But you're still burned."

"Oh," she said, looking down at her arm. "Well, I didn't think of it. Maybe next time."

Te Ruk opened his mouth to speak, then closed it.

Ny Auv stood. "No time like the present," he said as if commenting on a tunnel draft. And together, they stood.

o

Vo Jie considered how rare it was that all four of them had been outland before. There were camps full of miners, living day to day within a quick walk to the outland's edge, that considered whether it was even real.

Gu Non's wounds had disappeared, and though no one commented on it, Vo Jie reminded herself mages were perfectly allowed to use magic whenever they chose. Or, if there were restrictions, a simple miner wouldn't know them. She couldn't help but think of her own wound, but she didn't know how much magic each of them held in reserve, and didn't think they should waste it.

Ny Auv had seen the wound, of course, as they'd

become a bit friendly. Oh, who was she kidding. There was much more than physicality in their connection. But, as priests had their assignments, and she was just a miner who probably earned herself an unspoken death sentence, she held no hope for a future in it. None she'd allow herself to think about.

Though Gu Non's skin had healed, her hair remained asymmetric, shaved to one side and full on the other. Though unallowed by code, Vo Jie conceded that she wore it well.

Appearance was not their concern, not for any of them as they walked. Gu Non had more difficulty outland than she'd had in the mines, and she offered no explanation for it. Te Ruk awkwardly tried to comfort the younger mage, as Vo Jie now thought of her, but his awkward pats and comments left her silent, mostly, staring upward at the embattled dome as if it were going to crash down on them.

It was in Ny Auv's grasp where the girl finally found some comfort, silently allowing him to pull her small fingers into his own wrinkled hands, though saying nothing of it. Vo Jie watched them as they walked, a tiny smile on her face.

She expected some type of scene to be made as the odd group approached the Temple. Instead, he spoke a few words to the man at the entrance, and soon they were wearing clean, custom-fit clothes, and each offered a large plate of savory cakes with a rich oil sauce. Gu Non was wrapping hers into a napkin, which Vo Jie recognized as one Te Ruk had given her, and readying to stuff it into her bag.

"Gu Non," she said. "Gu Non."

Begrudgingly, she looked up.

"Allow yourself this one meal. If we can take food back, we'll take different food. This is made fresh," she noted. It was. "It won't keep." Again, that was true. It was part of her own justification for not pressing it into balls and stacking them in her own pocket.

After staring at her a long while, Gu Non relented, allowing herself a bite.

Even Ny Auv had not eaten so well since being in the mine, and so they leaned back in the wide, solid chairs, each at a loss for words, but knowing this peace could not last.

"We've pressed our time enough," Ny Auv finally said. Pausing for a moment then shrugging, he lifted the plate to lick off the remaining oil. Grinning, Gu Non followed him. Vo Jie shook her head as if too proper to join, but the fact was, she'd made sure to absorb hers into the cake. She saw Te Ruk's plate was similarly clean, and he smiled. It was nice to see it.

Again, Vo Jie was surprised that no one stopped them as Ny Auv guided the group toward the library. He finally addressed it, as if reading her mind. "Clan Temple prefers individual communications, not announcements and message chains like clan Mine. Word here spreads like your mage visits—one space at a time. Yet, it always spreads. And so eventually someone who decides we should not be here will decide to do something about it, after they discuss it for a lengthy while. Until then, I am relying wholly on their total lack of forewarning, and their vast curiosity in what

I am doing here with a mage and two, as they will see you, miners."

"But what about Gu Non? She escaped with magic!" Hadn't he considered it?

Ny Auv only laughed. "It is more than likely that whoever saw this is still considering whether their comforts will be taken for mentioning it. And, if they've described her, she has changed her hair since then. He swung two fingers in her direction.

Such a simple thing, Vo Jie realized. Miners never changed their hair. This would at least cause doubt whether she had been here before.

"Don't misunderstand. We aren't safe here." He glanced around. "But I figured we'd have a better chance with my acting confident in seniority than I would acting like there was a reason for suspicion."

"What did you tell them?" Gu Non asked.

"I said there was a spiritual crisis in the mine, and that the lady and the mage were leaders there, the child your charge. I thought the texts here would help. And about those," he lowered his voice, "we should appear solemn as we approach."

Vo Jie continued to marvel at the serenity of the temple as they followed Ny Auv through to the large central space. It was a forced serenity, she understood. One could not live here, no matter how loyal to their clan, and not see outland in shambles beyond its walls.

The raised ceilings impacted her the most. Ceilings were the most difficult stones to mine, and so the mine was built with low passages and low rooms. If there was enough room to stand and swing tools, it was tall enough. So, despite being familiar with the expansive heights of the outland, somehow seeing spaces raised in an inside context awed her even more.

And then they reached the library.

When she first saw the number of books in the library—and at this point she was really just beyond surprise—her heart fell, considering that there could be no method by which to read these countless books, especially without knowing what they sought.

"It's not as many as it looks," he said, his voice low. "Each priest provides a study, to prove their faith and knowledge. I've read many of them; they read the same. They quote Lord's Book, in its various forms, and they speak with passion of the future."

"Then," Gu Non interrupted, "which speak of the past?"

"Very few. And those almost in coded terms. I suspect any volumes with clear accounts were destroyed. Perhaps even with good intent, believed to be false accounts. But I've spent many nights here, trying not to be noticed, and there are some you might find of interest. This way."

He led them to a nook less impressive than the others, smaller shelves of books which showed their age. On further inspection, their quality was better. The lettering seemed too consistent for shaking hands, and the bindings were strong. Yet, there was no gilding on these. They were plain.

Te Ruk could not read well, and while Vo Jie could, she

was no match for the complexity of the texts here. With Ny Auv's agreement, they sat back and listened to the other two as Ny Auv browsed the books and Gu Non directed him. Vo Jie continued to glance around, wondering when they'd be interrupted. It was a remote corner of the room, and they stayed out of sight. Yet, she couldn't relax as time continued to pass.

"Read that again," Gu Non interrupted. "Please."

"And of the three, when Lord remained—"

"Who are the three?" Gu Non sat up.

"I admit, I've read this one before, but that point didn't strike me."

"The three," she mused. "Well, Lord is one. Enemy is one. Maybe Betrayer? But Betrayer came in later."

"Later than what?" he asked. Now Vo Jie and Te Ruk were both again listening. She caught Te Ruk's eyes.

"I don't know. But there was something going on. Something important. Before Betrayer was a part of it. Go back. Go back to when he was talking about service to Lord. That kind of boring part. I feel like we missed something there."

Ny Auv flipped back, and read on for a while. Gu Non stopped him again.

"Lord's trials made us stronger? Why are they Lord's trials?" She paused, appearing to think. "Look, they can't know they are Lord's trials unless there was a time without them. Maybe a time before Lord." She tapped the table. "Yes, the world was too difficult then. The wood, the winds. I think . . . I think Lord was doing it all."

"Doing what?"

"Making their life hard, for the . . . emotions." She rubbed her temples, looking very much not like a child. "Lord was using the Varr, like a resource. They were mining us. But then Lord and Enemy fought, because of Betrayer, and that's when the everstorm started. And Lord made the dome and then left. Oh, it's so confusing. I'm seeing pieces, but I can't connect it."

"Ahem," a throat cleared behind them.

"Ny Auv Temple, Chief Pe Fal Temple requests your presence. Immediately."

Ny Auv stood, and Vo Jie watched in admiration as he dropped the book as he rose, sliding it behind the table where Gu Non was seated. He held his hands forward. "Then let us leave." They all stood, following Ny Auv out through the main library space and into the hall.

"I know the way," he said to the man, turning to walk toward a large door.

The messenger made a rude-ish noise, and let them go, returning to say something to the people at the front as their group turned around a corner.

"Follow me," Ny Auv whispered. "And don't stop for anyone."

15 You Betrayed Us

Apparently, that vision was of Lord farming the Varr like they were grain. Putting them through trials to feed from their emotions. The purpose had to be their emotions: the magic was centered on them. Maybe Lord didn't have magic either; they just used the core fragments same as she did.

And if people didn't want her thinking things like this, well, maybe they should never have lied to her about the magic. And then they shouldn't have let that turd-hearted Ri Wid bruise her face just because she did what she wanted. What made him in charge of her anyway? She didn't accept it.

The more they walked on, the madder she got. She kept the book clutched in her arms, and Lord themself would have to stop anyone who tried to take it from her.

They left out some back passage of the Temple, and no one spoke. No one stopped. They kept walking what seemed like a long time, somewhat back in the direction of the mountain, but not toward it, she noted, until the structures were small in the distance. They walked through the leaning wood poles, which she now realized used to be the legs of those tall plants. This made her sad and she wondered whether any were left alive.

Mad now, and sad too, and frustrated and it was a good thing she wasn't touching a core fragment. Except, those emotions were already in her. Like a shield of her own. It was always the first time feeling each that was the worst. No, not the worst. The most shock.

She'd want to try another emotion soon. When she could. She wasn't sure which was best.

Finally, Ny Auv stopped. Without saying anything about it, he eased down behind a grouping of broken walls. Or at least that's what Ny Auv called the narrow shapes of stuck-together stone. Gu Non had never seen walls with two sides before. Not ones that were made from the stone, rather than chipped from it.

The priest didn't say a word, either, just groaned and rubbed his feet. Vo Jie sat near them, reaching slowly toward hers. Te Ruk plopped down a little farther away, staring off.

"What are the chances someone will look here for us?" she asked, deciding she might as well sit too. She didn't set the book down, though.

"Low, I think," Ny Auv answered. "While the area under the dome is not so large, and heavily taken for crops, it still has plenty of nooks, and since we're able to move within it, a full search would take a great deal of resources. It would also raise questions, and trust me, those are not so popular."

Gu Non snorted.

"What about clan Mage?" Vo Jie asked. "Clan Mage, could they use magic to search for us?"

"They could," Gu Non answered, before Te Ruk had time to respond. "But they wouldn't. Not unless necessary."

"Because of the core?" Vo Jie asked.

That was part of it. Magic used the core, and clan Mage was dwindling by the shift, it seemed like, listening to Vo Jie. But use of the core seemed to have a lot of skill to it too, and she'd never met a full-up mage. Sorry, Te Ruk was ok after all but probably not a mage master. Either way, she didn't think that was the biggest reason. And maybe they had some saved away. Maybe the clan Mage Chief had a whole closet of fragments somewhere.

"Yeah, but I think there's a bigger reason." She glanced at Te Ruk, hoping he'd accept the apology-in-advance. "They don't want the mages to understand the magic. I'm convinced of it. What they do, make the dome, clean the air, it's all sort of basic. Te Ruk?" The older man was still avoiding her. "You were taught to think about protection only, right? And told not to think about other things?" That was her theory.

He nodded, clearly still not comfortable with discussing the magic in the open like this.

"Ow!" The reaction shot out, though not on purpose. Lord's voice had returned, like a stabbing in her mind.

Protect them. We must protect them.

Yes, she was aware of that. She tried to pull herself back. Through the voices and the shouts of the Varr in her vision, the others clouded out again. Like falling back into the deep bathing pool, she felt like it took a few good pushes to come out again to the surface. There, there they were. Te Ruk was talking, perhaps. Oh, he was explaining that the magic gets into your mind. That seemed private; Gu Non could talk for herself.

"As she said," he was explaining, "we keep our mind as blank as we can of other thoughts. Without years of that training before even touching a fragment, she went right in. I can't imagine what it's like for her."

"Ugh, I'm right here," Gu Non complained, regaining herself a little. Well, if she was getting Te Ruk to stop being a secret-man who repeated lies, maybe that was worth it. "Anyway, that's true. The magic gives back whatever emotions you put into it." She tried to sit up, but had to keep her hands massaging her head for just a while longer. Then she put her palms on the ground and sat, pushing her legs to each side. Trying to connect back again, she wiggled her toes.

They betrayed us.

"So here's what I think, now from the books and from Lord's voice." The priest still clearly wasn't used to her talking about Lord in her head, but he was going to have to get used to it. He'd brought himself into this. Or Vo Jie had. Who knew. She didn't.

Her first theory was probably the most controversial. But with the stabbing in her mind, she didn't have the energy to worry about that.

"Lord was not always here," she said. "I mean, I don't know if they have regular age or not, but they were not always with the Varr. They are not 'everything' like some people say. They are a separate being. With some really intense thoughts," she added.

"And Enemy didn't used to be called Enemy. Well, none

of these are real names, I mean who calls themself 'Lord?'
But now that they got in a fight, Lord only remembers
Enemy by that name."

"Or that idea," Te Ruk interrupted. She cut him a glare.

"So Lord and Enemy were together, like I was telling
you before. And they agreed to protect some power source,
or a charge or something. But Enemy let Betrayer know
some kind of secret, and clearly by that name you know
what Lord thinks about them. I don't know what happened
to Betrayer, but Lord and Enemy got in a big fight. And
that's the everstorm."

She pointed up. It was right there, after all, crackling
and crashing against the dome in distant rumbles.

"But here's what I'm realizing. Before the fight, Lord
brought the Varr into their whole situation. And . . . they
bothered us, like with trials and storms, to make us feel sad
and scared and sometimes even happy. Then Lord used our
emotions as some sort of food. See, that part they left out
of their story."

The stabbing intensified, and Lord was rambling again
about Enemy.

Enemy can never be forgiven! Enemy told Betrayer!

"Stop it!" Gu Non shouted, standing up. "You did!
You left that part out. Enemy betrayed you but maybe you
shouldn't have been using people for food in the meantime!
Maybe I'd betray you too!"

She sat back down, ignoring the faces of her friends.
Well, surefine, that was a little much. Put Lord in their
heads and see what they shout out.

"Don't be afraid," Te Ruk murmured. "We won't leave you."

What? What had he said?

Lord had latched onto that, too. Fear was circling in her mind now, maybe feeding off whatever magic still floated around in her. Fear was one thing she'd tried so hard to keep away. If she thought of fear, she thought of Da Eel, crying in the mine. Being smacked by Ri Wid. And maybe never seeing her little brother again.

Or maybe she'd be the one to never come back, and he'd worry about her forever. And Ma Mav would cry, and Ri Wid would laugh. Or maybe Ri Wid would take advantage of Ma Mav, and she'd have no choice, to protect Da Eel.

Fear made awful, scary stories like that, and Gu Non tried to push them away.

But the fear was overtaking her, and the others were still talking, and Vo Jie was tapping her shoulder, and now she was lying down. "I'm sorry," she whispered. "I'm sorry, I have to see."

Da Eel. I'm scared. I'm scared for you.

No! Don't do this to me!

Nobody pushed things on Gu Non. And so she pushed it right back. Forcing her hand down, she grasped a fragment into her fingers, and held it tight. So tight. No one was prying that out, even if there was shouting somewhere. The blue light shot out from her, and they moved away.

What were you afraid of, Lord?

The thoughts and vision snapped together this time.

Almost. Sometimes the voices were ahead and sometimes they were slow, like a miner that couldn't keep up with the walking line. But they were the same thing. A place, or a time, or something. And Gu Non was filled with fear, and so was Lord.

Enemy had returned, but Enemy was much more powerful now. Gu Non couldn't see them, not specifically, but there was a sense, moving toward them in the depths, out even by the star, of a massive, powerful being. Enemy had not looked like this before. They were so powerful now.

They deserved it, Lord. I agree with you.

This voice rang in her head, like every pot in the mind all clanging at once. This was new. This was not Lord. Lord's reply felt like a whisper in comparison.

Are they in you now? They are part of you?

They always should have been! Your way was not better! Your way was not right! Tradition exists for reasons, Lord. You only saw yourself. Not the reasons. You should have known better. I should have stopped you. Betrayer was right, too. But now Betrayer is gone!

I am Betrayer! I am Enemy! I am Ours!

There was anger, also, rage, betrayal, sadness, desperation, *bitterness*. They were all there, but like a tight wrap pulling them all in was fear. *Fear. Fear. Fear.*

Enemy was powerful now, now that they had consumed Betrayer. More powerful than Lord. Lord could not consume a being so powerful. Especially not when Lord considered what Enemy was made of.

There was no way to win.

No way except to die.

I am afraid to die.

I will stop you. I will stop you. I will do anything left. Anything I can. It will not be easy for you. They will help me.

I am afraid.

"Gu Non!" Te Ruk had pushed past the others, and was over top of her now, blocking the sight of the everstorm. Pulling her shoulders, smacking her ears.

"Get off of me!" Gu Non sat up and knocked Te Ruk forward, where he tumbled back against the scruffy outland dirt. She pointed her glowing finger at him, lowering when she realized it looked like she was threatening him. Well, she just wanted him off.

Her heart raced as the light faded from her hand. Ny Auv and Vo Jie were seated together, arms around each other. And Te Ruk had stood up, brushing dirt from his clothes and muttering under his breath.

"Fear? Why'd you go for fear?" Te Ruk was shouting in her face.

"How do you know what I did?"

"I could feel it from here! What the ever were you so afraid of?"

So much power now! Foul power! How could you do this? How can you live like this?

"Not me! Lord! I saw another piece, at least until you interrupted me. Why'd you interrupt me? Lord was afraid. He was afraid to die. Enemy came back, really powerful, like they killed Betrayer and it made Enemy more powerful. They couldn't win against Enemy like that. They knew they were going to die. So they did something, just to, I don't know, to resist, I guess."

Te Ruk crumpled back down into a crossed-leg seat. "So?"

Her head pounded and she could barely keep her mind in this world. She wasn't feeling like guessing his meaning. "I don't know what you're asking."

"Did Lord . . . die?" He said it with pain, and hazy, Gu Non remembered they did not speak of death. But he asked it again. "Is Lord dead now?"

"What? Lord? Oh. Well, they were sure they would. But, if they're dead, and Enemy made the everstorm to kill them, then . . . what's the everstorm still here for?"

"They can't be dead," Vo Jie whispered. "If they're dead, who will stop the everstorm?"

Gu Non didn't want to say it this time, but maybe they were all going to die.

Maybe that's why she didn't think about fear.

16 Strong as Clan

Vo Jie stirred. With nighttime upon them, they'd decided to sleep in the relative softness of the outland dirt. She saw Gu Non's shape creeping off. Though she never rose so quickly these days, she managed to follow not too far behind.

"Gu Non," she whispered.

The girl turned around. "Can I get some privacy, please? Oh, you think I'm running away. No, not this time. I promise." She waved her napkin in the air, and embarrassed, Vo Jie crept back to where the others still slept.

Ny Auv was snoring rather loudly, and Te Ruk sprawled out like a mineroot. She gazed with fondness at the snoring priest. Just as she'd finally forced herself to admit she was in love with the man, she'd also forced herself to remember it wouldn't matter. They'd both disobeyed their clan; without access to food or supplies, they couldn't just go on out here. Nor could they return. She didn't know what would happen, but for giving Gu Non a chance, she knew it was worth it.

At least they were old. She worried about the children. Oh, Te Ruk was no child, but at her age it wasn't much of a difference. What life could they lead? Te Ruk had been seen with them disobeying an order from the priests; it would be hard to invent a story around that. And Gu Non had burned her way out of controlled labor just to steal a book from the Temple?

These were simply things that didn't happen.

But, that had been Gu Non's point in the first place. She sighed.

The star was growing now in the sky, and Vo Jie couldn't remember the last time she'd watched it rise. There was nothing like the color of it. There were so few colors in the mine. Gray of stone, and deep blue of the core. Blue of the mage light. The smokey gold light of oil lamps.

Here, even with the constant gray of the everstorm, and Lord's Dome casting an amber hue in the spots where light broke through, there were still colors she otherwise wouldn't see. A hint of soft red. Rays of peach. Specks of almost white. She strained to find hints of that color as the star's light rose, trying to imagine what it would have looked like without the dome.

She continued to imagine it as they got up and prepared to leave, as it took her mind from the other questions. The other pain. Not knowing where to go, or where to hide, it was Gu Non who suggested the mountain. "No one walks on the mountain, except on the passes to the mine. That way, we can truly hide." Vo Jie did consider whether Gu Non expected to sneak back into the mine for anything. At this point, she was putting her faith in her hands.

What could she give Gu Non now that the magic could not?

As they walked, Gu Non became more open about the emotions. About her plan.

"The magic focuses on emotions," she explained. "And, I'm not saying what it's supposed to be or how it works. I just know what I've done with it." Spoken like someone used to being corrected. It was always that way in the mines. And so Vo Jie did not correct her.

"The mages use protection. That's how they keep the dome up. They touch the core fragments and think about the dome. Probably inside the furnace. Which isn't one, of course, though there's probably like, a little stove for biscuits. Since no one goes there, and no one would question it, I'm almost sure that's where they do it."

Te Ruk's face twisted; Vo Jie guessed he'd not yet been there.

"It was the first one I used too. I thought Te Ruk was going to attack me with magic for threatening him, so I asked Lord to protect me. Zap, there's a big bubble, and I was able to get away. Gu Non's Dome!" She chuckled.

Vo Jie was glad to see her spirits up. Though, it could be a way of coping. They were all surprisingly upbeat; focused on figuring out what to do now, mostly because none of them wanted to think about what might happen otherwise. The darkness of that disturbed her, and she tried to focus on Gu Non's explanation.

"Then I tried bitterness, because, well, that's personal. I tried bitterness, and that's when I learned that Lord had failed at something, and they were so, so bitter about it. We're always told Lord protects us. And they'll return to save us. We've never talked about Lord being bitter. I didn't ask enough questions then, so I just knew they were upset. I didn't really understand why.

"Then I went to the Temple. The first time. I didn't think I was focusing on an emotion then, but I must have been, because I got out really fast." Gu Non gestured with her fingers, holding them still for a moment before moving on. "And then that got me in controlled labor. I told you what happened there. That was all completely on purpose."

She glanced back over her shoulder. "Maybe not on purpose, but, well once I realized it I didn't stop. That was anger. I was mad. Mad at everything and so I didn't use very much magic there. I didn't need to."

Vo Jie shuddered a little trying to think what she meant by that.

"Lord had as much rage as I did, too. We were feeding off each other, I guess. They were so mad about what Enemy and Betrayer had done, well, really mad. Except, the anger wasn't as much at Betrayer. It was all at Enemy. If Enemy hadn't told Betrayer the secret, there wouldn't be anything to betray. If that makes sense."

It made perfect sense, Vo Jie thought, more than a little jarred to be relating to Lord's clan troubles.

"Next was when— Well, ok, this was the time I did it on purpose. I was in my room, and I tried to practice. Except, I didn't pick the emotion this time. It sort of picked me. Well, maybe that's not on purpose either. I don't know, this is all sounding like a bunch of accidents."

She smiled a sad but charmed smile, realizing the room she was bragging about was the clan Chief storage closet. And what Gu Non had done was no accident. Yet, she didn't interrupt.

"That time, it was like, being desperate. And that's when things got really serious in my mind. That's when, you know," she shrugged back at Vo Jie, "Lord's desperation about what had happened." Her shoulders fell, and she didn't look back. "I don't want to talk about that either.

"And then, of course you know about the fear. Lord was going to die." Gu Non didn't need to say more. God or not, the fear of death did not need to be explained to Vo Jie. To the others, though, it had been a shock to hear them all using the word. Acknowledging its presence. She wondered whether that brought them more fear.

Vo Jie, she'd rather understand it. It was the unknown she feared. The inevitable didn't give her much choice.

"So that's my problem!" Gu Non sounded almost cheerful. *Coping,* Vo Jie reminded herself.

"What's the problem?" Te Ruk didn't ever seem shy about asking her these things directly. Well, he was as much a part of this now as any of them, she reminded herself. Whether he'd wanted to be or not. She stopped, then moved forward again. No, he'd brought Gu Non the fragments. That had been his choice. She watched the man, hopping up a low sequence of rocks.

"The problem is, we know all sorts about what Lord is feeling about *the resource* Betrayer used, but no one has figured out what *the resource* is."

Oh. Would that change things? If they knew? She wasn't sure.

Ny Auv spoke next. She'd almost forgotten he was there, he'd stayed to the back and not said much.

"You have diverged greatly from the core teachings of the Temple."

Was he lecturing her?

"I spent decades in and out the Temple, repeating to all in my path that we must trust in Lord's love for us. Love. Hope. His Return. The joy in which we may rest our weary minds. And it makes me curious, that for the cloth the Temple has lain to cover the idea that Lord could represent negativity, you have done the opposite. To you, Lord is only pain. Fear. Desperation. What type of being knows no joy?"

She didn't expect Gu Non to plop right down on the rocks.

"Are you well enough?" Te Ruk worried. "Don't you need time?"

"I need answers," she grumbled, reaching for another fragment.

How many was she carrying?

"What are you trying?" Te Ruk whispered.

Without opening her eyes, she answered. "Love."

Vo Jie kept her gaze on Gu Non.

Honestly, the girl looked like she was doing a morning stretch. It was remarkably unimpressive. When she opened her eyes, she was staring down at her hands. The stone was still there.

"It isn't the same. I couldn't find any love at all. And . . .

I don't even believe that can be true. It is either different for them, or something I couldn't understand. There were memories. Hints of light. It was all I could see." She sat up taller. "Here. I'll try again. Joy."

This one clearly worked. The blue emanated from her, and Gu Non writhed in her seat, murmuring words Vo Jie could not understand. Yet it was not as intense as before, and it didn't have the sense of joy, not from what Vo Jie could discern.

Gu Non opened her eyes. The fragment had depleted, and her eyes were again unsteady. Vo Jie would try to convince her to wait before trying again.

"Their joy is in power. They draw the power in. Eat it, somehow. When they do, they grow larger. I guess like how Enemy consumed Betrayer."

"That's their joy?" Te Ruk sort of choked the words. "They eat each other?"

Lord's blessing. She took that immediately back. Vo Jie would not be requesting Lord's blessing again. By the look she exchanged with Ny Auv, they were on the same checksheet.

Perhaps they should still talk this through while they had the chance, but Gu Non's glow hadn't subsided, and she appeared to be struggling somehow.

"She's not relating to it enough," Te Ruk said. "Gu Non, you need to channel it off. Think about protection. Make a bubble. Something. You know, something not too intense." He sort of half-grinned, though Vo Jie didn't think it was truly humor.

"Vo Jie," Ny Auv was whispering to her. "May I tell her about—" he pointed at her arm. "I think you need to decide quickly."

Oh, well, if it would help. "Sure," she said.

"Gu Non, please listen. Vo Jie has an old wound on her arm. There." He continued to point. "Could you heal it for her? With Lord's help?"

She didn't know whether Gu Non would rise, or touch her, or what might happen. Gu Non did not answer, but closed her eyes. A sensation filled her, and an immense pain lifted. One so severe she no longer understood how she'd been living with it—and immediately knew she could not bear it again. She lowered her shirt, not worried about the others, and removed the bandage, with the stain gone too. She saw her skin, brought whole again. Vo Jie had no room for tears, but maybe she cried inside.

Wasting good cloth was a terrible offense, but no one complained as she took the bandage, rolled it in a ball, and heaved it as far as she could, back down the mountain. Gu Non seemed to calm, and she whispered something Vo Jie did not catch. Te Ruk and Ny Auv both nodded.

"Now we rest?" Te Ruk asked.

"I can't yet," Gu Non said. "Thinking of love and joy, it didn't connect with Lord, but it's made me upset. For Da Eel." Her voice sounded younger now, like a smaller child. "I need to go back in and check on him. Will you wait here?"

Vo Jie considered this. "May I talk with Ny Auv first? Please?"

Gu Non nodded.

They stepped away, turning around a boulder to not be seen by the others. She had no idea whether the mages were sensing them here, but she'd always been of the mind that those who chose to pry could not be her concern.

"I'm nervous to send her back in," she said. "Her control is slipping, like before. I'm sure you can see it, as I do, in her eyes. But is that our choice?"

For a moment, she worried Ny Auv hadn't been listening. Then he answered. "There is a word in an old text that I think is pronounced, 'enslaved'. It means under the control of another and not by choice. By my measure, her young life was spent as such, maybe ours as well." He paused, as though fighting his own fear with his defiance. "And if what she says is true, then we were enslaved by Lord as well. While they were here. And now this." He pointed upward, to the everstorm, which loomed much closer here on the mountain than it had below on the outland plain. "It discussed an alternative. A life of choice, of chosen connections, choosing to be mindful of all. An old book, wedged away. I have never forgotten it. It called this idea, 'free'. And so I think . . . She is better free."

That was a lot to consider, except for now it was not. "What if I give her the choice, then. She can go, or I can." Ny Auv may have wanted to argue, but she kept her expression clear. She had choice as well.

"I love you, Vo Jie. If I had a core fragment in my grasp, I would clutch it and burn forever of the brightest blue, burning forever from my thoughts of you."

Vo Jie smiled, letting the darkness rest just one more moment. "I'm still going to offer her the choice. And if there is ever a place for this love, I promise you—I will join you in it."

She wanted to touch him. Embrace him. Join him in a long kiss. In more. But it was a fiction, and she could not indulge it. A deepness in his gaze, he swung his hand forward. "After you," he whispered.

Walking back to where the kids waited, she sat in front of Gu Non. "I will offer you a choice. If you check on him, we will wait here. Or I'll go in and check, while you rest. I recommend that you let me help you. I promise I'll tell you the truth of what I find."

"But you don't have magic," she said. "You won't be as safe."

"Child, I have my own magic. Decades of life will at least grant you that."

Gu Non drew a breath. "Thank you, Chief Vo Jie Mine. I'll wait here. And rest. Please, please look out for Da Eel."

She nodded, first to Gu Non, then Te Ruk. Then Ny Auv. And then she left.

17 More Precious than Eternity

Vo Jie returned from the mines faster than Gu Non thought she would. Though, she'd rested a good amount, here on the side of the mountain. Not for the fun of it. And not just to keep her word to Vo Jie. But to get off of empty, so she could continue to fight.

Maybe to some people, learning a story didn't feel like fighting. But when your whole life had been revealed to be a lie, then no fight seemed more important than the one for the truth.

During her times awake, Ny Auv had read to her from the book. Though it didn't help her right now, he'd insisted on teaching her some of the symbols. She'd written the signs for "hello" in front of Te Ruk while he slept. He'd smiled pretty big at that, and they'd both laughed. That was nice.

And Vo Jie looked surprised to come back and find them all laughing together. Maybe it had to do with being outside of the mountain. It was much harder to laugh on the inside.

She stopped laughing when she saw Vo Jie's face.

"I'm sorry, Gu Non, I have bad news," she said. "Da Eel has been commissioned."

Gu Non sat up, but Vo Jie held out a hand, like she needed to finish first.

"I had him in quarantine, but one of the Schedulers decided I'd been missing too long. My name is not being spoken, and the room is already occupied by the new Chief. Someone checked on Da Eel, found him of sound health, and released him. Your Boss, I won't say his name either, immediately made the request. Probably to punish you. I won't lie to you, Gu Non. I'm sorry. But I urge you, don't give up now. Let's keep working. Let's find a way to help him."

Not wanting to hear another pisstalk word of this, Gu Non grabbed the book and ran, as fast as she could, toward the entrance to the mine. They shouted after her, and she ignored it. She was much faster than the older miner and priest, and more clever than Te Ruk, so she knew they wouldn't catch her. Finally, seeing the main tunnel that led into the mine, and the flattened path leading from it, she stopped.

Gu Non was used to busting through to places and figuring out what to do after that. But, with Da Eel's safety at risk, maybe she should think of a plan first. She knew she could find her crew. She could use the magic to protect Da Eel. She could take him away.

But, could she take the others away? What would happen to Ma Mav? Her siblings? What would happen to her crew? If other miners spoke her name, could they get punished by the new Chief?

Gu Non wondered if she knew what she was getting into. And maybe if Vo Jie had been replaced, maybe Te Ruk had been as well. Maybe a new mage was in his very-much-too-large room with four chairs. And maybe that mage would fight her. Maybe they'd have a mage battle and maybe she'd lose. What would happen to Da Eel then?

And out here, her friends. Who would take care of them? Te Ruk, she thought. Except, Te Ruk wasn't well. He hadn't been well, she realized, since all of this began.

When it was just Gu Non doing her own thing to save everyone it had seemed more easy. Be brave and save everyone. Now, it felt like there were more paths. Or maybe Lord's fear had crept into her blood now. But here she was, outside. And she'd even found people with a tiny bit of power who could help her. And now they were all here, on the outside, because of her.

Maybe she'd already failed.

The tremors started again inside of her. She understood now why Te Ruk used the fragments as a drug. It wasn't to feel good, it was to fight the overwhelming emotions that she couldn't ask to go away. Desperation. Fear. Now Lord's creepo sense of joy. She couldn't stop them from coming back. She couldn't just push them aside. Each one turned inside her like a storm, just adding to the mix of feelings her period was already dragging around.

Had Gu Non acted too soon? Had she failed?

Unable to bear the pressure, she slipped her hand inside her pocket, unwrapping Vo Jie's scrap fabric around another stone.

Lord had felt defeat too.

Enemy closed in, huger and more powerful than ever before. Their expanse was a universe in itself, stretching and circling. Lord would have had a chance to escape, if they'd been careful. If they'd been watching. But Enemy was here now, closing around, and there was no path Lord could take to avoid them. Lord was going to die.

Lord embraced their beings, knowing they would die too. That wasn't right. These were Lord's beings, they'd found them, not Enemy. Lord cared for their beings. These beings had been part of the best time of Lord's life. The life Enemy had taken from them. A life Enemy could have shared.

The beings, they could help. Yes, there was a way. A way for Lord to thwart Enemy. Power surged in their core.

Enemy was used to taking what they wanted. Not this time.

You can't have us.

Enemy closed in, in color and shape and endless power. And rather than offer them a literal final sting, they threw all their remaining energy into one thought: keeping Enemy away. From Lord. From their beings who would continue to protect them until there was nothing left to protect. And as Enemy's assault began and Lord's final spirit broke, they reached inside, and released a sphere of protection. They could not protect the fast beings, or the outside beings, or the ones already dead on their land. They protected a few, and hoped it would be enough. They hoped the beings would remember them well, remember their Lord.

Protect me.

And as Lord's life drew from their body, they crashed back against the land, thrusting deep into the soft stones, as others pushed up and over them, creating a large pointed peak. And over it, over the beings, in their last sight, the sphere took form, a golden color like the one who had been lost. Reminding Enemy, over and over and over again, what they took away.

Enemy, I will never forgive you.

The stone closed in, over them.

Gu Non expected the voice to continue. To cry and yell and howl of loss. But in this vision, Lord had died, and the vision ended as abruptly, leaving Gu Non shocked and sick and gasping for air. Lord had died. Died erecting the dome that protected the Varr. They would not return, they were right here. This mountain, it had been created by Lord's fall into the land.

The core is Lord's body.

She needed more time to think. Seeing the scene over and over in her mind, she wasn't ready to return to the others. She wasn't ready for their worried expressions, or the effort of explaining what she'd seen and felt. Or why she, as well as Lord, had failed. Instead, she hiked across the mountainside, the book clutched in her arms, with one specific goal in mind.

And as she reached the dome's edge, she saw the amber light close up. In front of her, the way her small bubble of protection had been. Not solid, but made of magic. And so, needing now to see what lay on the other side, she pushed through.

She could not breathe. She took in what she could, as long as she could withstand it: heat and smoke and death.

The world continued on beyond the confines of the dome. The land here was devoid of life or structure, beyond what the stone itself made. A land made of char, interrupted only by the flow of red-hot substance. Smoke rising up to meet the bombardment that continued from its every side.

Just as inside, the everstorm opened and closed, like a being itself. And as one path broke above her, Gu Non had to shield her face. For looking up, with her own eyes, she could also see the light: clear, plain light. Unmarred by fire or smoke or magic, light streamed down in a fan of ribbons from their star, still in place, still hovering as if waiting for them to return.

The sight, unlike anything she could have seen or imagined, filled her with joy. And if she was going to die here, standing in the everstorm, she could at least know that first she saw the light.

She would not die.

She couldn't breathe, and coughing, she stumbled back, pushing through the amber barrier and back inside the dome, back where the light was muted with gold and the everstorm an echoing rumble.

Overwhelmed, she slid to the ground, not familiar with the emotion beaming from her like that light, and she was almost out of fragments, but she took one more, the largest that she had left, and held it in both hands, as she rolled back onto the hard rock, its spikes poking her.

The emotion had a name: *Wonder.*

They had not meant to do it. They had not known

why such changes occurred; they were rare in these epochs, almost unknown. But Enemy was a special being, and they had drawn together. And when they had awoken, they saw the being between them that could not be.

Baby.

Ours.

Weak gods were always consumed; it was the way of things. The way of growth. But Lord saw nothing but wonder in the tiny shape that undulated before them. Nothing but future, and perfection, and everything that Lord could ever hope to be.

We could share them, Enemy said. That would be fair.

Consuming them was proper. That was tradition. Yet Lord could not do so, nor could they tell Enemy what they truly felt.

We must protect them.

So they told Enemy a new plan. Instead of consuming this small god, it would be better to feed them. To grow an ally. Maybe, then, when Ours was older, they could work together. Not just two, but three. Power in numbers, not in size.

Ours? Enemy laughed. You name them first, before consuming them?

Lord would not let Enemy consume them.

Over years they argued, Lord insisting their way was better. And maybe Enemy had a soft center for Lord after all, because when Lord flew away to an outer network and dragged Ours with them, Enemy allowed it. And then, Enemy visited, not yet speaking Ours' name, but interested in their progress. Lord had found the beings. Alone here, far away from most gods, they had claimed them, and through their dedication, Ours grew strong.

Enemy still did not like the plan. They did not like the beings.

Leave then, Lord said. Leave us. Live your existence far away.

○

Enemy told Betrayer about Ours.
Betrayer consumed them.
I will never forgive Enemy.

○

Gu Non's mind was cracking, just like the stones outside of the dome. Lord's last thoughts had been of protection. They said they were protecting the Varr, but they were protecting themself. Spiting Enemy.

It didn't matter. Gu Non felt like Lord. Felt like the everstorm was closing on her too. If she would die, she would die saving the Varr.

Lord did not own her. In life or in death.

No one owned Gu Non.

She was determined to save them.

Trying to return to the others, hoping they had stayed to wait for her, Gu Non stumbled ahead. But the magic was glowing harder now, and determination pressed on her.

Cursing, she forced herself to stop, to let this new emotion run its course.

Lord's story started to push into her mind. Determination to convince Enemy, or to avoid them, or any such thing.

"No!" Gu Non shouted. She was tired of Lord's past. Now she cared only for their future. Her people's future. Her friends. Her family. This charred, damaged land.

She turned the energy in her away from Lord and to herself. The determination gave her strength, and power, and she charged now, at great speed, over the rocks and toward her friends.

She ignored their faces of surprise and fear as she returned, the light no longer blue, but all colors. All the colors Gu Non had seen in the vision. They streamed from her, and she told the others what she had seen.

Lord and Enemy had a baby.

Because of Enemy, the baby was consumed. Killed.

Now Lord was dead. Their body was in the mountain, under Lord's Dome, where Enemy couldn't reach it.

Enemy was the everstorm. Enemy was still here.

And Enemy wanted them all.

18 Pray

It hadn't really been a difficult decision to stay where they were.

There wasn't much they could do to protect Gu Non anymore other than to be there to provide a foundation in the gaps where she lost her own. If she'd gone into the mine, well, Lord protect all of them. Maybe if enough time passed, they'd need to intervene. But for now, they'd agreed to stay here.

Gu Non had taken the book with her; Ny Auv complained about that more than a bit. But, he'd also conceded, she had a unique perspective the others couldn't imagine. It was better in her hands. Even if she couldn't read it.

Out of nowhere, the everstorm had picked up. The cracking intensified, and the light dimmed. The dome itself seemed to flicker. Gu Non was involved, Vo Jie was sure of it. She rocked back and forth, trying to sing, trying to do anything to distract herself from the tumult overhead.

So when Gu Non came stumbling back over the rocks with glowing eyes and emanating light in colors Vo Jie had never before seen and telling them Lord had a baby but they were both dead now, Vo Jie was glad her bottom was planted firmly on the ground.

"I think you need a break," was all Te Ruk had said, before leaving to refill Ny Auv's flask in the stream. They sat in silence, Gu Non still glowing, until he returned and handed it to her.

"Here, I've cleaned it for you."

Gu Non downed the water fairly quickly, and Vo Jie was relieved to see her glow was starting to fade.

There was just only so much glowing Vo Jie could take.

Yet the storm continued to intensify. And Gu Non's mind did not return as her natural color did. Vo Jie worried whether she could recover this time, whether her eyes would stop flitting in every direction or her words would start to reform in ways that made some sense.

Whether the dome was about to break around them.

Only Ny Auv seemed to be able to keep her talking, and he continued to speak to her in a calming voice, as much to keep drawing her to the present, Vo Jie suspected, than even to learn what she was trying to say.

"You are sure Lord is dead?"

As much as their lives had changed, she still couldn't get used to hearing such words. And it couldn't be easy for Ny Auv to say them, she realized. He was brave too, like Gu Non was. She rested a hand on his knee, and for a moment their eyes met. He turned back to Gu Non.

"Yes," she said. "Enemy killed them. Dead." Her eyes moved around.

"Stay here, Gu Non. We need you. What happened when Lord died?"

"They did not attack. They made the dome." She babbled a few more thoughts, ones they could not understand.

"Lord chose to make the dome, rather than to fight back?"

"Yes." Her eyes widened. "Not just protecting us. It felt . . . not about us. But we could not die." Again, she slipped into the nonsense words, and Ny Auv did not react, but only reached to hold her hands. She let him.

"Does Enemy want us to die?"

"I don't know. Don't know. Lord used us for power." Her eyes flicked. "Maybe Enemy— No, I don't know if they care. They want Lord's body."

Ny Auv began to stroke her hands, and she did not pull away.

"You said the Gods consume each other, for power, right?"

"Yes. They eat each other."

Vo Jie winced.

"So Enemy is here, making the everstorm. And they want . . . the core."

"Yes." Gu Non's head was starting to slump, and she slipped back into the babble. Te Ruk moved behind her, leaning her against him and whispering in her ear.

Ny Auv walked over to Vo Jie, and like a big child, rested his head on her chest. It was for show, of course—as she had no chair, he couldn't lean without knocking her over. She patted his thinning hair, and he sat back up.

"So I can curse to Lord now, right? If they're dead?" He looked away, guilt all over his face. "I believe her. So I'm making myself say it. I won't let myself run away scared. Or pretend I don't know. I can't."

Yes, Vo Jie herself had struggled with this sense of shock, when Gu Non had first approached her. Whatever change this child was experiencing, it wasn't the same as having the floor pulled from you after decades of living one way.

That didn't mean she wasn't going to try and change. The world may still need them yet.

"What do we do?" he asked. The storm cracked again, even louder than before.

Vo Jie appreciated his patient approach, but they must all see the storm intensifying. Their time may be running out. "Gu Non," she said sharply. Gu Non's head sprung back, but with the expression of an irritated child.

"Why is the storm worse now?"

This time, Gu Non's voice was clearer. "Enemy saw me outside the dome, I think. They're mad."

Enemy. But, it was obvious. Just—the exact opposite of everything she'd ever been taught. "Probably why I hadn't considered it," she murmured.

"What?" Ny Auv tilted his head.

"Ready for this?" She looked over at him. He just laughed.

"Ok, great. It's just a little blasphemy, is all. We need to pray to Enemy. I have an idea.

"Gu Non!" She sounded like she was scolding a slacking crew Boss, but she could see the girl struggling to stay with them.

"I need you to make an offer to Enemy. Do you have any more core?" Gu Non at first stared blankly, as if not understanding the request. When Vo Jie asked about the core, she nodded. "Use it. Use everything you have left. Repeat my words." Gu Non nodded, and somehow, Vo Jie believed that she understood her.

As Gu Non glowed, again in all the many colors, Vo Jie spoke, as if Enemy was seated among them. "Enemy! We have an offer for you!" She wasn't sure how this could work. Would Gu Non signal? Without any sign, she continued to speak.

"We will give Enemy the thing they want. All that remains of Lord. We will drop the dome, and Enemy can take all their power. If Enemy accepts, they must not hurt a single one of us. Then they must leave us alone. Leave this place forever."

Gu Non was twitching now, her eyes rolling around. Te Ruk held her like a baby, making soothing sounds and keeping her from hitting any of the rocks. Vo Jie tried not to think about it, for what else could she do now but continue?

Above them, the dome was cracking. Enemy's power had grown, and the mages could not hold it at this rate. The dome started to fade, to disappear in patches. Soot and black rock flew down around them, spitting down onto the mountainside. She didn't know if Enemy knew this. There was no time to let them learn.

"If Enemy does not accept, I, as Chief of the Varr, will command the entirety of our people against Enemy. We will hurt them, for what they have done to our Lord."

She almost said, "to us," but by the way Gu Non had

described it, that might not make the same impact. A charred rock fizzed down, dangerously near them.

"No!" Gu Non screamed, a horrible shrieking scream that must be hurting her throat. Now realizing that this could be working, for that could not have been Gu Non, Vo Jie sat higher, urgency pumping in her blood.

Yet, she didn't know what else to threaten. How could mere beings convince a God. A God who didn't care whether they lived or died.

Died.

If Vo Jie was going to die, there was something she wanted to say. If the others could be brave, she could be brave.

"I had a brother," she shouted, to whomever could hear. "His name was Lu Qoy. His name was Lu Qoy. He is dead now. My grief for him spans the universe."

Grief.

None of them had considered grief. It was a forbidden thought. Erased. Now, it tingled in Vo Jie's fingers. Was the magic in her too?

Gods consumed each other. But was there grief? Lord, withering away here, out of Enemy's reach. She tried to change her thoughts. How would that feel?

The emotions in the air crackled like static. Vo Jie tried not to think of Enemy as a God, but as another being. Hurt. Scared. She thought about everything Gu Non had told her, today and before. Vo Jie had spent a lifetime dealing with people. She understood them. What fueled them. What stopped them. How to convince them onward.

Sitting up, she spoke again with strength.

"We know that Lord hurt you, Enemy. We know they were powerful to you. That they should not have wasted their power. Both of your power. We also know Lord was wrong about you. You have honor. And so, you have heard my offer. Do not hurt us. Give us back our world. Leave us alone forever. And in exchange, you may consume Lord. You may take Lord's power, and know that Lord loved you."

Her voice cracked now, but she knew she had to finish.

"If Enemy does not take my offer, then we will consume Lord. We, their beings. I, as Chief of the Varr, will command every last being into the mountain and we will lay ourselves upon them and we will feed upon them, as they fed on us. We have tunnels surrounding them now. I know you can sense these. We will fill those tunnels and consume every last piece of Lord. We know that you will kill us after, but this is the cost of refusing our offer."

With alarm, she saw Gu Non now, seizing in Te Ruk's arms, with spittle on her lips. Ny Auv leaned over her, helplessly reaching out his arms, with no way to help, but unable to rescind the gesture. Her friends. Her lover. This had gone far enough. Sometimes, like with children or miners or puffed up crew Bosses, there was a time to make your point and then stop. *That is our offer. I will not say it again. Now, make your choice.*"

"Ny Auv," she commanded. "Prepare to order all Varr into the mine. Send out the call."

Enemy did not answer, but the wind intensified around

them. Howling so fast that they held each other, they dug their feet into the rocky surface and prayed to anyone at all that they would not fly away.

Vo Jie could not have spoken now, if she wanted. Acutely, she noted the wrinkled skin of Ny Auv's fingers, clutching her own. Softly, she said goodbye.

The wind grew, and it screamed, like a person's scream, and suddenly a feeling of nakedness emerged around them. Enemy was taking Lord. They'd accepted the deal. But, she realized her flaw. Enemy would not hurt them, but every miner would be crushed, by the mountain collapsing over its own void. They would die here, as the ground fell out beneath them.

"Gu Non! Help us!" she thought, straining to be heard over the wind, and feeling the words, inside her being. Emanating them, willing Gu Non to hear her. "Love! Not Lord's love! Your love! My love! Da Eel! Can you help Da Eel?"

Gu Non glowed brighter, and Vo Jie, through her squinting eyes, saw Te Ruk, thrusting several large fragments into Gu Non's hands, where, subconsciously, she clutched them. She grew brighter yet, colors streaming from her. A tremendous blast made Vo Jie spin, pulling her hand from Ny Auv's and she lifted it to shield her eyes as a crack formed in the center of the mountain, bubbles emerging from within. Hundreds of people, then more, then perhaps every miner still alive, rose into the sky, hovering calmly in a chaos of light and storm. A small burst of dark dots caught her eye, falling all in a sequence, from those farthest back.

Only then did she realize they were hovering too, the ground crumbling away beneath them. Time warped. It was forever, or it was a moment, it was all so hard to understand, and the air pinched in Vo Jie's chest. But as the land settled into a low slope of rubble, the bubbles floated down it, resting in the low fields at the base of what used to be the towering peak.

Finally, she crawled along the ground, searching for Gu Non. The child lay there, no bubble around her, and no longer glowing, but bathed in light.

She looked up, her eyes calm. Recognizing Vo Jie's face above her, Gu Non smiled.

"We can't go back to the mine," she said.

"No," Vo Jie agreed, "that we can't."

19 The Light

There wasn't much strength in her limbs, not even enough to stand. And so, assuring Vo Jie she was fine in a voice that made it clear she couldn't be stopped, she crept forward, almost dragging, until Te Ruk popped in ahead of her. "I found them," he said, pointing over to where Gu Non's family was gathered.

Ma Mav's arms were wrapped around herself, and she stood, blinking around at the strange, bright light, free of both Lord's Dome and the everstorm assailing it. Her siblings surrounded her, and her father, who gazed in confusion. She saw Ba Dos nearby, with his family too. He didn't see her yet, but he looked ok. Still worried, she scanned for Da Eel, then saw he was running toward her. He tossed an overlarge set of mining gloves to the ground.

"What did you do?" he asked, eyes as wide as she had seen them.

Gu Non laughed. "I fixed things." She reached up and pulled his little fingers into hers, feeling the chafed skin, unused to wearing the gloves. She wished she could heal them, but there was no more magic. "You don't have to go back there again. Actually, it doesn't exist! See, look! No mountain!" She was feeling more and more proud about that. Blowing up a whole mountain, that was pretty notable. "I'm just sorry I didn't fix it sooner. Here, go back to Ma Mav; she's worried and needs you right now. Tell her I'm ok and I'll be with her soon."

Arms still wobbling, she rolled back into the dirt, immediately rolling back on her side with a hand over her face, for the light was so bright now. That would take getting used to.

Her mind was empty now, but it didn't feel right, either. Not like before. Just like the mountain, whose blue core has ceased to exist, there were holes in Gu Non's mind too. Places where things had existed, then been taken. It felt too quiet, and it echoed, a lot like the mines.

She wasn't sure that was going to fix so easily.

People were all watching her, she noticed. Ny Auv was holding hands with Vo Jie. That was nice. She could tell they liked each other. And she supposed there was no going back for either of them, now. One couldn't really be a miner when the mountain was gone. And as for being a priest, it did seem all the gods had officially left.

She listened again in her mind. Yes, they were definitely gone. Maybe Vo Jie and Ny Auv could just be old together; she wasn't sure how things worked now.

For a moment, she thought of Enemy. She wondered what name Enemy gave themself. She felt it, for a moment, flickering in her thoughts, but it was too distant through the memories of Lord's magic, and the name slipped away. Oh, well. The thoughts she'd had of them in her mind were not evil. They were sincere. Jovial. Warm. Yet, this same god had killed and tortured the Varr.

A part of her felt like Lord on that. That it could never be forgiven.

And maybe a part of her thought, now that they were gone, promised never to return, that her thoughts were better focused on other things.

Enemy had changed again, now, just as they left. Enemy had consumed Lord, as well as Betrayer, meaning Enemy had also consumed their child together, the one Lord called Ours.

This was actually a whole lot of strange.

And as powerful as Enemy was now, were they, like, the most powerful god? Or still just a small one, struggling to find others to consume?

Gu Non had spent long years in the mine, but she was at least glad she wasn't a god.

Te Ruk had crouched down near her. "The outlanders are walking this way. We should go meet them. If you need to rest here, I'll find someone to stay with you." He hesitated. "I need to go, so I can explain things to my clan. They will be scared, if as I think it did, the fragments in the furnace disappeared."

"They did," she said. "I felt Enemy sensed those; they took them as well. I mean, you can check, but I'm pretty sure." Te Ruk glanced nervously down the hill. That's right, he said he had to go. They all did. "I might be able to stand," she said. "I just felt like jelly after—all of it."

Te Ruk laughed, though she wasn't sure what was so funny.

He offered her an arm, and she took it. One of her

friends, Ij Lok, saw her teetering, and came over to help. "I've just been through a bit," she told him. "If you could help me walk." Rising, she first turned to face the mountain. It was low now, still made of jagged rocks, but with a wide mouth over which water poured, falling through the air and splashing down into something that looked like it was turning into an outland lake.

Then, she realized, everything was outland now. So, then, a lake.

With her friends' help, she walked out, as long as it took, down the long slope, toward the point where the structures first came into view. As she walked, her steadiness returned, though her mind did not yet settle.

The outland people were not hidden in their structures now. They were out, in huge groups, some facing their way. She peered ahead, expectant. Perhaps she expected the outland people to rush to meet them. To embrace them and praise the ending of the everstorm.

Instead, they shouted. They ran. They shook objects in their hands.

And those were the people approaching. Among the structures and walls, people pushed and shoved. Someone had set something on fire.

Gu Non had no magic. And no strength.

Somewhere in her, she found something that was left, and she stumbled ahead, not quite able to run but close, heading straight toward the Temple. The gates were sealed shut and she could not break through, so turning again before the masses caught up to her, she ran around the huge walls, into an open area with benches and a raised platform, and large openings in the stone. She supposed these were windows, too.

She stood on the platform, calling out. "I am Gu Non! I ended the everstorm. Clan Temple, are you here? I need your help. Now! Please!"

At first, she thought there was no response, but then a stream of robed priests filed out of the main doors, walking and surrounding the platform. Soon, an older man, in such fancy robes that Gu Non could not have imagined them, walked out, each step slow and not looking like he worried for the slowness, joining her.

Someone was trying to push through the line of priests. She saw Ny Auv and Vo Jie, holding hands still. "Let them in," she shouted. She looked right at the older man, his face looking tiny within his shiny cloth robe and hood. "Please, tell them to let them in. Let them join me. He is a priest, too."

"I know who he is," the priest said, making several hand gestures, after which Vo Jie and Ny Auv were able to break through, joining her on the platform. Gu Non started to speak, but Ny Auv walked past her. He stopped, giving her a clear look. She nodded.

"My Chief," he said, bowing deeply. "I say not our clan, because it has effectively disbanded." That got people riled up, the ones that heard him, anyway. But the Chief raised his hand and they immediately quieted. "You can see the shape my friends and I are in. You see the mountain with your own eyes." He waved into the distance. "I was there. And so I have no reason to tell you anything but the truth."

Lord is dead, Gu Non thought.

"The everstorm has ended," Ny Auv said. "Just as Lord's Book said it would. Their nemesis has departed—" Ok, Gu Non was realizing this was a selective tale, but at least he wasn't making Lord a dude. "And now we are called to a greater light." He pointed upward.

"There will be time, in the many cycles to come, to discuss and understand what has happened. But now, in the scorching light of our star, with our well-being in peril and the expanse of our world burned and scarred, our energy is best spent saving what remains. As Lord's Book said we should. Fostering it. Growing, so that we may thrive. To reclaim our place. As spoken in Lord's Book, 'To serve me is to serve the light.' Look, Chief, above you, the light has come."

He turned to the crowd, speaking over the line of priests. "The light has returned. Can anyone deny this?" As the crowd noise erupted, Ny Auv moved closer to the Chief. Gu Non could still hear him. "Clan Temple has a new mission. If you will take it. We must lead in this confusing time. Comfort. Guide. Offer ourselves to all. We must serve tirelessly, helping expand the gardens and build homes for those without. There is no more magic. There is only us." His voice quieted some. "This is what I've been waiting for my whole life. I intend to lead. Will you?"

This was getting really fancy. Gu Non stepped forward, speaking directly to the Chief. "Can I say something?"

The man looked down at her as if confused. Ny Auv started to explain but she gave him a polite enough wave.

"Hi, so I'm Gu Non. I used the magic to end the ever-storm. Now, you tell me, am I making that up?"

The man didn't answer, but his brows rose.

"Ok, great. I'm not, and I think you should listen to me. I like what Ny Auv said. I agree. And I have a couple more things." Annoyed that Vo Jie and Ny Auv always had to hear *everything*, she leaned in, whispering toward the man, who bent down to hear.

They exchanged words. To her surprise, he nodded.

"Wait, one more thing," he said. "You must be the one who used magic in our library. Then came back again. I heard of it. The magic—is it really gone?"

Gu Non gave her answer. Then she stepped back.

The Chief moved forward, and the crowd quieted to hear.

"Repeat my words," the Chief commanded, and for each phrase he said, each of the gathered priests repeated the words back, loud so the crowds could hear.

"The light has returned."

"The light has returned," the priests repeated.

Gu Non still thought that was creepy, but at least it seemed to help calm people down.

"What we have worked for, all this time, has come to pass."

What?

"Now, we must work again. Old clans do not fit the contours of this new land. I decree a new charge, a group dedicated to service. Anyone who chooses to join us may apply. We are no longer he, but she, they, any, many, all, and none as well." This caused a bit of a stir, and Gu Non beamed like the bright star above them.

"We have no name, not for now, but if you choose to join us, please go to the Temple entrance."

Well, maybe the Temple was still a good name, Gu Non thought with a shrug.

"To everyone else, I ask for your calm as we gather and decide how best to move forward. All previous ranks are no more. All will have a voice." He waited for the rumble to subside.

"There is something I need to say. One more time." He looked at Gu Non, and she wasn't sure what this was about.

"Lord's blessing be with us."

"Lord's blessing be with us," the priests echoed.

"Lord's blessing be with us," the crowd repeated.

And with that, the priests broke out of their lines, walking through the crowds, asking how people were, comforting them, or just offering hugs. She heard one tell someone that he wasn't sure what would happen but for now, they should focus on helping each other.

Gu Non liked that message.

Beside her, Te Ruk was whispering. "Rejoice in the light," he said.

Gu Non sighed. "I'm up for some joys. But some stuff's gonna change."

20 A Land of Color

Vo Jie had a house built on the edge of what people now called the "domeline" – the boundary between the land that had previously been under the dome, and the charred lands beyond.

She and Ny Auv believed in a future for the vast areas outside of the domeline. It had been their home once, and they believed it could be again. Water streams now crossed the parched land, and the air was breathable again. With Lord's Dome gone, the sky had begun to reform a new dome, one that tempered the star's light. This was not made of magic, it seemed, but of the air itself, or maybe also of water, as water now sometimes fell from it.

The falling water was not unpleasant. Vo Jie liked the feel of it on her face and hands.

The soil outside of the domeline seemed even better than that inside, and some seeds had even been found pushing through it with curly sprouts. Vo Jie had brought her own to the area beyond Vo Jie and Ny Auv's cozy home, and a little garden had begun to grow. Of plants to eat and plants to just be plants.

In the library, they'd found a book on taller plants called trees, and Vo Jie believed those could grow again, from old seeds and roots, and she'd planted a ring of them around their house.

Some were even growing between the rough rocks of what used to be the mountain, now a hill of rubble striped by a series of waterfalls, leading down to a large lake. Vo Jie didn't visit the rubble; she'd had enough rocks, but she did like visiting the lake sometimes, tending to the plants there as she gazed across at the waterfalls in the distance.

She was sharing what she learned with the farmers, whose crops were already increasing in both size and also variety. She avoided the old council members, the ones who'd not cared that her previous services were not from preference, but rather from determination to help her clan.

They were easy to avoid; there were so many others now interested in learning how to tend to the land and the plants beginning, again, to cover it. Her only condition now was that, in exchange for her help, they agreed to sow and tend as many non-edible plants as farmed. So far, they'd embraced the offer with gladness. And so, the lands were, day by day, turning green and brown and blue, and all shades of color.

Te Ruk had built his own home not too far away; they'd stayed friends, and he came in to check on them a few times a day, which people now all associated with the periods of light when the star was overhead. He didn't call it checking in, of course, but Vo Jie and Ny Auv weren't getting any younger, and she knew checking in when she saw it.

The former mage had built himself a small house and a large forge, dedicating himself to the craft of blacksmithing.

Despite the demand for them, he rarely made tools, and usually only as favors for good causes. He preferred to make objects just meant to be beautiful, and for his distribution of them, everyone made sure he had what he needed. And so the young man was often under the high roof of his forge, laced with green vines, pounding out the curves of door handles, garden rails, and a variety of lovely items Vo Jie would never have thought possible.

He led counseling sessions, too, down at the old Temple. Said he had a lot to work through, and if he did, others would too. Many of the old clan Mage had taken up to participating along with the miners, though Vo Jie herself hadn't had the spirit to join them. Maybe one of these days.

The former clan Temple Chief had turned into one impressive town planner, enough that there was almost no resistance to putting them in charge of the rebuilding effort. With the restrictions lifted, even if they were their own clan's restrictions, the Chief had immediately announced themself as "they" and then got right to work. A variety of people had joined the new effort, and the city was already looking better and stronger by the day.

It was easier to delay broader issues of governance with basic needs still being met, but those were in work, too. Representatives from the former clans had identified those they most trusted to help lead, and while it was not without contention, slowly, plans were being put in place for a new council of sorts to help plan community-wide services and ensure all had what they needed. And surely, resolve disputes, Vo Jie knew. And Vo Jie kept an eye on those proposed; there'd be a few she'd have words about if needed be.

Not all the former outlanders understood the difference in trauma that the miners had experienced, and not just those who had experienced controlled labor, something Vo Jie was set to see never instituted again. Even their rescue held its own pain. The complete change in environment was jarring enough, but when the mountain had collapsed, everything a miner hadn't had on them had been destroyed.

Vo Jie at least had her locket, hanging around her neck, with Lu Qoy's hair still inside it. She rested her hand on the cool metal sometimes, knowing how much he would have loved this world. And so, she tried to live it for both of them.

The door opened, and Ny Auv walked in. She stifled a chuckle. Having left his less-practical priest robes behind, the man was still not used to wearing pants. He didn't understand that they hung, once belted, much like a robe. There was no need to pull them to meet the armpits. Well, she'd told him once before, and she wasn't going to keep tapping on it.

They leaned in together for a kiss. Vo Jie drew her hand up and rested it on his cheek. "It is a good day when you are here."

His face twitching a little, he managed to smile.

She touched the edge of it. "I was just on my way to visit Gu Non. Would you like to go?"

"I would," he said, edging over to a chair, "but my back

is protesting again. Please send her my best. Tell her I'll be by for a lesson soon."

The schools hadn't formally started up yet, but the new building was almost done. In the meantime, those who could read had been generous about finding someone new to teach. By far, reading had become everyone's favorite pastime, even more than the ability to play running, sweeping games in the broad outland fields.

Stopping to rub Ny Auv's back, and allowing him the slightly uncomfortable groans that accompanied it, she patted his shoulders and headed for the door.

She was glad Gu Non's mother had agreed to live out this way, though she hadn't wanted to be so close to the domeline as Vo Jie was. As for Gu Non, she'd almost gone to live by herself. And while she was certainly capable, Vo Jie was glad she'd decided to stay a while. Though the reason had been Da Eel, of course, she was glad that it allowed Gu Non not to give up on youth so fast.

But the young would never hear such a thing, so she was just glad she'd stayed.

The house was one of the largest in the area, and Vo Jie had made sure, with the help of Pe Fal, that it was also the nicest and most comfortable. And that Gu Non had her own room. The others either didn't understand or fully believe the role that Gu Non had had in saving them all. Maybe, for Gu Non's sake, that was just as well.

Te Ruk had taken a special interest in Gu Non's father, trying to offer him counseling and care. He'd admitted, privately, the man might be beyond help. He'd turned to harsh reactions for too long and his temper flared too easily. But the young blacksmith hadn't yet given up, a kindness Vo Jie appreciated.

She tapped her metal walking stick against the large structure, then stepped back, because the door opened outward.

"Vo Jie," she heard a voice say, and the door opened, Gu Non and little Da Eel almost tumbling through it. Though her skin was healed, Gu Non had continued to keep her hair shaved on the side it had burned, and let it grow further out on the other. Vo Jie hadn't thought too much of it, until she'd seen some older people with the same look, walking through the fledgling market. Vo Jie's hair was beyond much styling, but she admitted being a little jealous of the ability to try such fun, new things.

There had been so many rules in the mine. Thinking about it always brought her to a place of guilt. Maybe she did need to try that counseling.

"Well, let her in," Gu Non's mother said from an inside doorway, offering her the miner's signal of entrance.

Vo Jie smiled and signaled back, stepping into the broad stone room, light streaming through its overlarge windows.

"How are you?" she asked Gu Non, accepting the offered seat at the large dining table. It had been hard to find solid boards this long, but several of the old buildings had been salvaged to aid all the new construction, and Vo Jie had seen to it Gu Non got a table large enough for the whole family. Not knowing Vo Jie's role in it, only recently had Gu Non stopped reminding her this table was larger than any that had ever existed in the mine.

"I'm fine," she said.

Vo Jie tilted her head.

"I'm working on it. But that's surefine, I mean at least I'm not down there anymore."

"You might need to work on it a while, Gu Non." She tried to think how to say this. "Our eyes look ahead, to the future, with the help of our minds. But our minds are built on our own pasts. Each new step," she continued, "requires a step we've already taken."

"What?" Gu Non cut a side glance to her brother.

Da Eel chuckled. "She's saying it's ok if old things still hurt. You can still have a nice day."

I said what? Well, sure.

"I suppose I was trying to say, don't be embarrassed if you need help."

"Oh, I'm not."

"Well, great." Vo Jie glanced around. "You know, there's something I keep forgetting to tell you."

"Ok."

"I wanted to thank you for all that you did. I'm sure I've said it in passing and around town, but I want to say it officially. Thank you for stepping forward, when you were alone doing it. All of this, we owe it to you."

"Aw, sure. But, Vo Jie, you helped me too. And I went to you in the first place because I knew you'd listen." Distracted, Gu Non was already flinging something at Da Eel, who was laughing again.

Realizing what Gu Non had said touched her, but she'd need to think about it more later—now there was something else she had to say. Then, maybe they could drop it for a while. Go back to talking about plants and construction and other interesting things. "Gu Non, there's something else. When you saved the miners, you saved all of them." That included the bullies, and even Ri Wid, though she didn't want to say his name. "I want you to know how much I admire that."

"I know. I mean, of course. Just like you did."

"What?" Vo Jie had no clue what she meant.

"When you were Chief. You helped everyone too. Not just people you liked, right?"

"I did my best," Vo Jie said. This was all exhausting; why had she wanted to bring it up again? She sat back in her chair.

"I've decided something." Gu Non stood up. "I'm going to be a mage." From the other room, Vo Jie heard Gu Non's mother stop and listen.

"A mage?" She didn't know what else to say. Whether the child was well. There was no magic.

"Well, I kept on thinking about it. And we've worked it all through. Da Eel is really good with puzzles. And he can do things that make it look like one thing is happening when another one really is. He's not as good at talking, though. I'm better at talking. So we're thinking maybe we already worked enough orders-work, you know in the mines, for a while. And maybe now our job can be going around and doing tricks, and calling it magic, and maybe making people smile while they are building everything up."

She grinned, her eyes alight. "What do you think?"

"I think I'd like to see the show. Will I be allowed in?"

Gu Non laughed, and the new mage's laughter filled the room, like all the colors in the world. Vo Jie placed her hand over her necklace.

It would be a long way ahead. But at least they were free.

○

The End

About the Author

E.D.E. Bell (she/e) loves fantasy fiction and enjoys blending classic and modern elements. A passionate vegan and earnest progressive, she feels strongly about issues related to equality and compassion. Her works often explore conceptions of identity and community, including themes of friendship, family, and connection. She lives in Ferndale, Michigan, where she writes stories and revels in garlic. You can follow her adventures at edebell.com.